ASSASSIN'S CREED

ASSASSIN'S CREED

A WALK THROUGH HISTORY (1189–1868)

A VISUAL GUIDE

RICK BARBA

Scholastic Inc.

An Insight Editions Book

CONTENTS

INTRODUCTION

Artwork of the Thames River from *Assassin's Creed: Syndicate*. In 1864, just a few years before the game begins, a summer of nauseating stench known as the Great Stink led to the construction of two enormous sewers along the Thames.

The Assassin's Creed series of action-adventure video games from Ubisoft has become one of the most popular franchises in gaming history. The main reason, of course, is that they're simply fun to play. Each title features gripping action based on fiendishly clever stealth and movement mechanics (parkour, anyone?), all unfolding across meticulously rendered open-world environments. Each tale is well told and well acted, with gameplay smoothly integrated into a story filled with compelling characters. Ubisoft has received much-deserved critical praise for taking interactive gaming to higher levels of narrative sophistication.

IMPORTANT NOTE: Please be aware that we've organized our chapters according to the strict chronology of history. Thus our historical overview of *Assassin's Creed III* (American Revolution) drops down in our timeline to fall behind *Assassin's Creed IV: Black Flag* (Golden Age of Piracy) and *Assassin's Creed: Rogue* (Seven Years' War)—even though *Assassin's Creed III* was actually released before the other two titles.

But one other aspect of Assassin's Creed has truly captivated fans of the series: the painstakingly accurate historical setting of each story. Whether it's the Third Crusade, the Italian Renaissance, the Ottoman Empire of the sixteenth century, the Golden Age of Piracy, the Seven Years' War, the American or French Revolutions, or Victorian London, each era has been carefully, lovingly recreated, down to the smallest details. Ubisoft's design teams are so dedicated to historical accuracy, in fact, that they have actual historians on staff.

Since you're here, you're obviously a fan of the series. We assume that, while playing one of the games, you've wondered at some point: *Is that really the way it was back then? Did that actually happen?* This book takes a closer look at the "true history" behind the settings, events, and characters of each Assassin's Creed game.

ASSASSINS VS. TEMPLARS

YOU MAY BE SURPRISED TO LEARN that both of the factions depicted as mortal foes in the games actually existed in history. At the time of the Third Crusade, the Assassins—a secret society within the Nizari Shiite sect of Islam—had been active in Masyaf and other mountain strongholds for many years. Their skill in the art of assassination was widely known and greatly feared. And by the twelfth century, the Knights Templar had become an elite military order operating in Crusader-conquered lands and elsewhere. Associated with the Catholic papacy, the Templars were quite powerful and well financed during that era. However, the "ancient rivalry" between the two groups as depicted in the games is entirely fictional.

CHAPTER 1

THE THIRD CRUSADE

◼

The original *Assassin's Creed* set the tone for the series by creating a compelling portrait of a fictional protagonist painted on the background of actual history. The story sends Desmond Miles back into his "ancestral memory" of Altaïr Ibn-La'Ahad, a disgraced member of the Assassin Brotherhood working to redeem himself during the Third Crusade in the late twelfth century.

ALTAÏR IBN-LA'AHAD

Trained in the fortress at Masyaf in the late 1100s, Altaïr rises through the ranks to become a Master Assassin and eventually, a Mentor. Enigmatic and driven by a strong sense of duty, Altaïr's almost mystical quality could be seen as a representation of this time period. Altaïr is the author of the Codex—his autobiography, which includes studies on the Apple of Eden and assassination techniques—and his leadership and wisdom are still felt by modern Assassins. Altaïr is the protagonist of the first *Assassin's Creed* game, the co-protagonist of *Assassin's Creed: Revelations,* and is briefly playable in *Assassin's Creed II.*

HISTORICAL OVERVIEW

Concept of a marketplace in front of the fortress in Acre. During the Third Crusade, this castle was the headquarters of the Hospitaller Order. The first floor is still intact today, although some areas have not yet been excavated.

The Third Crusade was a military expedition of European troops that embarked in 1189 to conquer what was known as the "Holy Land," an area with great spiritual significance to three major religions: Christianity, Judaism, and Islam. Also known as the Kings' Crusade, the campaign began as a joint call to arms by the English and French monarchs. Those two mortal enemies had been fighting each other for years. But when a Muslim army captured Jerusalem in 1187, a wave of fervor swept across Europe, bringing together previously warring kingdoms in a united effort to regain the lost lands.

THE RISE OF SALADIN

The city of Jerusalem and the surrounding region had been Muslim-governed for centuries before Pope Urban II ordered the First Crusade in 1096 to reclaim what was called the "Holy Land." This first crusader army conquered Jerusalem, bringing it under Christian control for the first time in 450 years. For 88 years afterward, the crusader-created Kingdom of Jerusalem remained allied to the European monarchies and the Catholic Church; it also served as the headquarters of several powerful military orders, including the Knights Hospitaller and the Knights Templar, founded to protect crusader lands.

But by the late twelfth century, a brilliant young Muslim leader named Saladin was consolidating power in Syria and Egypt and turning his attention to Palestine. By 1187, Saladin had been proclaimed Sultan (the formal term for a Muslim sovereign) and amassed a powerful army, which he led to a series of conquests across the Holy Land that included the recapture of Jerusalem from the crusaders.

CALL TO THE CROSS: THREE KINGS AND AN EMPEROR

It took both King Richard the Lionheart of England and France's King Philip more than a year to muster up the troops, ships, and equipment they needed for their expedition. Meanwhile, the Holy Roman Emperor, Frederick Barbarossa, immediately "took up the cross" (as heeding the call to Crusade was called). The Holy Roman Empire was an ever-shifting collection of feudal states in Central Europe, including at times the Kingdoms of Germany, Bohemia, Burgundy, and Italy. Barbarossa left for the Holy Land a full year before his counterparts from France and England, leading an immense German army that purportedly included twenty thousand mounted knights. Unfortunately, while crossing a river in the mountains of present-day Turkey, Barbarossa's horse slipped and the great leader was drowned in the swift current. His sudden death threw his troops into disarray. Much of the grief-stricken army dispersed and returned home to Germany. Only a fraction of the original force—about five thousand soldiers—managed to arrive in the Holy Land.

ABOVE: Concept art of the South Kingdom
RIGHT: Character art of the Sultan Saladin

ACRE AND ARSUF

In the spring of 1191, all forces of the Third Crusade—French, English, and the remnants of Barbarossa's German army, led now by Leopold V of Austria—finally converged outside Acre, a vital port on the northern coastal plain. Fully understanding its importance as a gateway to Jerusalem and the entire region, Saladin defended Acre aggressively. But Richard the Lionheart's arrival tipped the scales in favor of the crusader army. Not only were his English knights amongst the finest troops in the field, but his keen understanding of military strategy—and, in this particular case, of siege tactics—gave the crusaders an important advantage.

Richard oversaw the deployment of powerful siege weapons against Acre's fortifications, punching great holes in the city walls. The city fell just a few days later—a surprising development after the months of protracted siege. From there, Richard led the Crusade south toward the important port city of Jaffa. Saladin's army shadowed his move, and finally launched a full attack near the fortress town of Arsuf. (See "The Battle of Arsuf" later in this chapter.) The crusader ranks held firm, then launched a devastating counterattack that routed Saladin's troops.

BELOW: The port of Acre

OPPOSITE TOP: Another concept of the Hospitallers' fortress. The castle had two floors built around a central court with an underground water basin and sewage system.

OPPOSITE BOTTOM: King Richard the Lionheart with the crusader army

AFTERMATH: THE TREATY OF JAFFA

Acre and Arsuf were resounding victories for Richard. But, abandoned by his French and German allies, he realized that taking Jerusalem was too risky, despite his strong position in the coastal cities. His numbers were just too small. If Jerusalem fell, the vastly superior numbers of Saladin's combined forces in the surrounding region could seal off the city and make it difficult to defend. Thus Richard decided to pursue a treaty that could lock in the gains made during the campaign. On September 2, 1192, Saladin and Richard agreed to a three-year truce. The agreement left Jerusalem under Saladin's control but guaranteed safe passage of pilgrims of all faiths into Jerusalem to worship at their holy sites. It also left most of the coast and its port cities under crusader control. Richard returned to England a month after the treaty was signed.

HISTORICAL CHARACTERS

◄ KING RICHARD I

Renowned as a fearsome warrior and military mastermind, Richard I of England was widely known as "Richard the Lionheart." The son of King Henry II and Eleanor of Aquitaine, Richard displayed advanced martial skills and political acumen at a young age. At six foot four, he towered over most men of his day, and his courage, combat skills, and sense of chivalry were legendary. Although Richard ruled as king of England for only ten years (1189–1199), his heroic stature grew large during that decade, as attested by his popular nickname.

The statue of Richard I near Westminster Palace in London. The horse has one foreleg in the air to signify that Richard died from battle wounds during a siege in France.

Unmarried members of the Knights Templars wore the traditional white cloak with a red cross. Married members of the Order wore a black or brown cloak with a red cross.

ROBERT DE SABLÉ / KNIGHTS TEMPLAR ▶

Robert de Sablé was a trusted lieutenant of Richard the Lionheart; Richard rewarded Sablé's loyalty by helping him attain the coveted post of Grand Master of the Knights Templar. At around 60 years old, he was a relatively elderly man (by medieval standards) during the Third Crusade. (He appears much younger in the game!) At the Battle of Arsuf, his Knights Templar proved to be a key catalyst in the crusader victory. Sablé died of old age in 1193.

In 1192 Al-Mualim sent out Assassins dressed as Christian monks to kill the king-elect of Jerusalem. The assassination was successful, and even now no one knows who contracted the hit or why.

AL MUALIM (RASHID AD-DIN SINAN) / THE ASSASSINS

Rashid ad-Din Sinan, known in his time as the "Old Man of the Mountain," led the Nizari, a religious sect based in the mountains of Syria during the Third Crusade. Known as the Assassins, the Nizari were feared by crusader and Muslim leaders alike.

As the Third Crusade unfolded, the Assassins' services were greatly desired by both sides. For years, Sinan and the Muslim leader Saladin had been bitter enemies. But one night, during the sultan's siege of the Nizari's Masyaf stronghold, a lone intruder slipped into Saladin's heavily guarded tent while the mighty sultan slept. Instead of murdering Saladin, the would-be killer left a note, pinned by a poisoned dagger, calling for a halt to the siege. The Assassin then slipped out, undetected. His identity was never revealed, but some sources suggest it was Rashid ad-Din Sinan himself. The next day, a shaken Saladin called off the siege and sought an alliance with Sinan and his Assassins.

THE ASSASSINS were well known for their ability to eliminate prominent targets in broad daylight, often in public settings. They occupied a few mountain fortresses (including Masyaf, as depicted in the game). But the Assassins were largely an underground movement, operating throughout the region as spies and stealthy killers. Their weapon of choice: a poison-tipped dagger.

Although not quite as barbaric as shown in this concept art, medical practices during the Third Crusade often did more harm than good, sometimes even killing the patient.

◄ GARNIER DE NABLUS (NAPLOUSE) / KNIGHTS HOSPITALLER

At the time of the Third Crusade, Garnier de Nablus was Grand Master of the Knights Hospitaller. (In the game, his surname is spelled "Naplouse.") Nablus led his Hospitaller units during the Battle of Arsuf, and, in fact, he was personally responsible for the dramatic charge that ensured victory for the crusaders. The historical record paints him as a respected leader, somewhat different from the sadistic, ruthless "doctor" portrayed in the game.

Stonework featuring the cross of the Knights Hospitaller. Unlike the Templar Cross, this symbol has pointed arrows at the end of each arm.

◄ WILLIAM V, MARQUESS OF MONTFERRAT

William V, known as "William the Old," was a deeply loyal and highly respected military leader, loved by his troops, who participated in both the Second and Third Crusades. William served as Marquess of Montferrat for more than fifty years, and was likely in his early eighties by the time of the Third Crusade. But he was vigorous enough to participate in the disastrous Battle of Hattin in 1187, which solidified Saladin's control of the Holy Land. William ended up a prisoner during that clash, but was released a year later, and died of natural causes in the summer of 1191.

MASTER SIBRAND / TEUTONIC KNIGHTS ►

Sibrand was the founder of the hospital that became the birthplace of the Teutonic Knights. As the crusaders' long, brutal Siege of Acre dragged on before Richard the Lionheart arrived, Sibrand's field hospital served the German troops posted there. After Acre finally fell, Sibrand moved the hospital into the city, and the facility evolved into the permanent base of the Teutonic Knights. A few years later, the military order was formally recognized, with Sibrand named its first Grand Master.

KEY LOCATIONS, LANDMARKS, AND EVENTS

MASYAF

At the time of the Third Crusade, the fortress town of Masyaf—located in Jabal Ansariyah, the coastal mountain range of Syria—served as headquarters of the Nizari religious sect and their elite Assassins unit. The Nizari, led by Rashid ad-Din Sinan, controlled a number of mountain strongholds, but Masyaf was their headquarters. Before the Crusade, the sultan Saladin set about subduing all of his Muslim competitors in Syria, and sought to include Masyaf in his string of consolidating conquests. But a near-assassination scare convinced the sultan that pursuing a truce with the Masyaf-based Nizari was a better course of action.

A photo of the ruins of Masyaf

JERUSALEM

One of the oldest cities known to man, Jerusalem has been at the heart of conflict for thousands of years. It is considered one of the holiest places on earth by three major religions—a fact that partly explains its long, often tormented history: In its lifetime, Jerusalem has been attacked fifty-two times, besieged twenty-three times, captured or recaptured forty-four times, and entirely destroyed at least twice. At the time of the Third Crusade, it was the largest city in the Holy Land, but its symbolic and religious importance far outstripped any strategic or economic value.

RIGHT: The Apple of Eden was kept in this container atop the Ark of the Covenant.

BELOW: Concept of the Old City of Jerusalem

THE ARK OF THE COVENANT

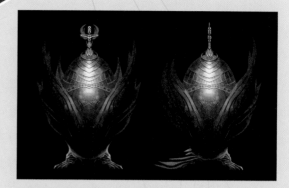

ACCORDING TO BIBLICAL ACCOUNTS, the Ark of the Covenant was a golden chest or casing that contained the stone tablets on which the Ten Commandments were inscribed and handed down to Moses on Mount Sinai. This chest was said to be stored in Solomon's Temple in Jerusalem, secured in a special inner room called the Holy of Holies.

Richard's army marches towards Jaffa.

THE BATTLE OF ARSUF

After the fall of Acre, Philip II and Leopold V abruptly left the Holy Land with their armies, leaving Richard I as the sole commander of the remaining expeditionary forces. Even with a shrunken army, he proved to be a shrewd tactician. As Richard marched his troops south from Acre along the seacoast toward his next target, the port city of Jaffa, his well-trained knights kept Saladin's large mounted raiding parties at bay. Crusader crossbows inflicted fearsome damage on Saladin's light cavalry.

THE ARROWS OF SALADIN'S ARCHERS would bounce off the English infantry's heavy armor, or lodge harmlessly. One eyewitness reported seeing crusader soldiers marching down the coast with multiple arrows sticking out of their armored backs!

SALADIN'S ASSAULT

Saladin knew that control of Jaffa would give Richard the base he needed to launch his assault on Jerusalem. He also saw that his skirmishing harassment was not working—the crusader march was relentless. So, thirty miles north of Jaffa, Saladin chose a wooded spot near the fortress town of Arsuf to commit his full army to an assault. At first glance, the attack seemed overwhelming—Saladin's army outnumbered Richard's nearly three to one! But as the first Muslim waves burst from the trees and struck the crusader lines, Richard ordered his men to maintain tight formations. The crusaders had the superior armor and weapons, so the English king could afford to wait for the right moment to unleash his heavy mounted knights in a counterattack.

THE HOSPITALLERS' CHARGE

The "right moment" came sooner than Richard planned. The king had placed his elite units in the front and rear of his army. Robert de Sablé led the Knights Templar at the vanguard (front) of the column, while the Knights Hospitaller under Garnier de Nablus brought up the rear. (You'll recognize those names as major characters in *Assassin's Creed*.) As the battle intensified, Saladin shifted his greatest attack pressure to the rear, where the Hospitallers held their ground, some even marching backward to keep their faces and shields toward the enemy while moving with the crusader column. Saladin himself rode forward into the close combat, trying to goad the knights into breaking their formation.

For hours, Garnier de Nablus pleaded with King Richard to release his knights to attack. But Richard repeatedly ordered the Grand Master to hold tight. Finally, Nablus could take it no more. He burst through his own line of infantry and rode wildly into his enemy's ranks. Seeing this, the rest of the Knights Hospitaller swiftly followed. Richard knew he could wait no longer, and signaled for a general charge. Within minutes, the entire crusader army was rushing toward the enemy in a full frontal assault. Saladin's ranks broke, and the retreat turned into a full running rout. Although Saladin was eventually able to regroup, he realized that his light, swift army was not equipped to engage the crusaders in a full-scale pitched battle.

Read more about de Sablé (right) on page 15 and de Nablus (left) on page 18.

In medieval warfare, cavalry charges were often used to create panic and confusion among the enemy's infantry.

CHAPTER 2

THE ITALIAN RENAISSANCE

■

This chapter covers the history behind two games in the Assassin's Creed series. Both *Assassin's Creed II* and *Assassin's Creed: Brotherhood* are set in late fifteenth-century or early sixteenth-century Italy, during the great flowering of culture—and corruption and murder and intrigue—known as the Italian Renaissance. Both games plunge Desmond Miles into the ancestral memory of Ezio Auditore da Firenze, a young Florentine aristocrat and an Assassin Master.

EZIO AUDITORE DA FIRENZE

Assassin's Creed II introduced Ezio, who would go on to star in *Assassin's Creed: Brotherhood and Revelations* as well. Born into a wealthy family in Florence at the height of the Italian Renaissance, Ezio's flamboyant and charismatic personality is a perfect fit for the high drama and culture of the time period. In his quest to avenge the death of his father and brothers, Ezio rebuilds the Assassin Brotherhood and frees Italy from Templar control.

HISTORICAL OVERVIEW

The Italian Renaissance was a period of stark contrasts and, as one historian puts it, of "glorious upheaval." Great wealth generated by powerful ruling families such as the Medicis, the Borgias, and the Sforzas seeded the gardens of creativity in the fifteenth-century city-states of the Italian peninsula. But that wealth also spawned a turbulent, often violent political landscape.

PATRONAGE AND DESPOTISM

Politically, Renaissance Italy was an unstable, shifting mosaic of states. Alliances were cold-blooded, and betrayals were common. Rich strongmen who could afford mercenary armies rose quickly then fell just as fast. The Catholic Church's popes waged greedy, acquisitive wars against Italian city-states. Meanwhile, Spain, France, and the Holy Roman Empire fought one another and the regional principalities for control of trade and commerce. The raw, cynical wielding of power by ruthless men and women in central Italy was explored by the shrewd observer Niccolò Machiavelli in his masterwork of political philosophy, *The Prince*, which ultimately gave us the term "Machiavellian" to describe such behavior.

On the other hand, in places like Florence, Rome, Venice, Milan, and Naples, great artists enjoyed plentiful patronage, producing works commissioned by the powerful elites. The Catholic Church funded a great deal of magnificent art, but there was often crossover between the secular (nonreligious) and clerical seats of power. Ultimately, four Medicis served as pope, as did two Borgias (including Rodrigo Borgia, as Pope Alexander VI).

Thus, Renaissance giants such as Michelangelo, Leonardo da Vinci, Raphael, and Botticelli largely owed their brilliant careers to the generosity of rich and powerful patrons. Most great works of the period—the Sistine Chapel, the Medici villa murals, the Vatican's Raphael Rooms, plus hundreds of friezes and frescoes in dozens of palaces, courts, and cathedrals—were commissioned either by the Church or by fabulously wealthy bankers and merchants, some of whom ruled their Italian principalities as new-age princes.

ABOVE: Young artists in the funeral chapel of the Medici.

BELOW: Leonardo da Vinci's workshop. The final version shown in-game would also include books, drawings, and the flying machine.

HISTORICAL CHARACTERS

◄ LORENZO DE' MEDICI

Historians generally refer to Lorenzo de' Medici as a brilliant statesman and the most important ruler of the Medici clan. His father, Piero di Cosimo, had become one of the richest men in Europe, leveraging ownership of the Medici Bank into absolute political control of Florence. But in doing so he created many enemies. When Cosimo died in 1469, Lorenzo was only twenty, and rival Florentine families planned to wrest control from the young Medici heir. But Lorenzo proved to be a savvy ruler and diplomat, using bribes, subtle threats, strategic marriages, and political surrogates to earn the nickname "Lorenzo the Magnificent." An assassination attempt by rivals (see "The Pazzi Conspiracy" later in this chapter) only solidified his position of power. His court in Florence included most of the great artists of the day; Michelangelo lived in the Medici family home for five years.

LEONARDO DA VINCI ►

If anybody embodied Renaissance ideals, it was Leonardo da Vinci. Painter, engineer, sculptor, anatomist, inventor, cartographer, scientist, writer— in many ways, da Vinci seemed superhuman. In 1502, he was briefly employed by Cesare Borgia as his chief military engineer and architect. He designed fortifications and created remarkably accurate, detailed maps for his patron.

NOTE: The Assassin's Creed design teams drew a lot of inspiration from Leonardo da Vinci's sketches when they developed the flying machine, tanks, and various weapons for the games. In *Assassin's Creed II*, Leonardo was even responsible for various crucial upgrades for Ezio's hidden blade and vambrace.

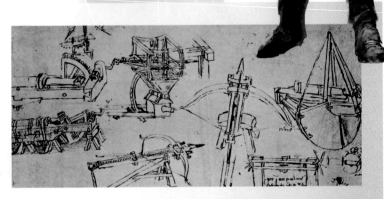

NICCOLÒ MACHIAVELLI ▶

Often called the "prototypical Renaissance man" because of his wide range of skills and interests, Niccolò Machiavelli became an important political philosopher, humanist, and writer . . . yet spent much of his adult life in Florence as a government official and envoy. He was by all accounts capable, and a savvy negotiator on diplomatic missions. But Machiavelli would go on to author *The Prince*, one of the most influential works in the history of political writing. Many of Machiavelli's keenest insights in that book were based on his direct observations of the brutal but effective ruling precepts of the Borgia family— in particular, Cesare Borgia, who many believe was the model for the literary "Prince."

◀ GIROLAMO SAVONAROLA

Much of High Renaissance art took classical Greek and Roman themes as subjects—"pagan themes," in the eyes of religious purists like Girolamo Savonarola. In the late fifteenth century, the Dominican friar started a movement that demonized pagan art and also targeted the decadence of wealth, corruption in the Church, and the evils of despotic rulers like the Medici family. He claimed to have prophetic visions, and attracted throngs of followers. Unfortunately, Savonarola's reformers soon turned into radical vigilantes patrolling the streets. (See "The Bonfires of the Vanities" later in this chapter.) Within a few years, Savonarola's claims had grown so extreme and puritanical that popular opinion turned against him. Pope Alexander VI excommunicated the friar from the Church and, not long after, he was tried and executed for heresy.

◄ BARTOLOMEO D'ALVIANO

Based in Venice, Bartolomeo d'Alviano was a *condottiero* (head of a mercenary army) and an enemy of the Borgias. In 1509, he led a Venetian force against an invading French army under King Louis XII. D'Alviano's Venetians were soundly defeated at the Battle of Agnadello, losing more than half their soldiers in a vicious three-hour assault. D'Alviano himself was wounded and captured. He remained a French prisoner for four long years, until 1513.

THIS PATRICIAN FAMILY from the Republic of Venice was one of the city's most influential houses. In 1485, Marco Barbarigo (below right) was crowned doge of Venice after the previous doge, Giovanni Mocenigo, was poisoned. Barbarigo didn't last long, however. He died less than a year later in a "fatal wrangle" with other nobles during a senate meeting. Barbarigo was succeeded by his brother Agostino (below left) . . . who may or may not have been one of the nobles involved in the "wrangle."

A painting created for *Assassin's Creed II* showing Marco Barbarigo stealing another man's wife.

Cesare's utter daring at political maneuvering made him one of the most feared men in Italy.

CESARE BORGIA

Cesare Borgia was the illegitimate son of Pope Alexander VI. He was highly educated, skilled at politics and war, and a charming man with diplomatic gifts as well. Originally destined for a career in the Catholic Church—at eighteen, he'd already been appointed as a cardinal—his life took a turn when his brother Giovanni, commander of the Papal Army, was killed in a never-solved mystery. (Cesare was a natural suspect.) Cesare resigned as cardinal—the first person ever to do so—and took his brother's military post. Using a mix of diplomacy, siege, and bribery, Cesare steadily brought large portions of central and northern Italy under his control. During this period he gained the grudging admiration of Niccolò Machiavelli, who chronicled Cesare Borgia's political methods in *The Prince*.

Unfortunately for Borgia, his father's death in 1503 resulted in the new papacy of Julius II, a bitter, longtime enemy of the Borgia family. First, Julius stripped Cesare Borgia of his titles. Then Borgia was imprisoned while the Vatican took control of his lands. He managed to escape and join King John III of Navarre in 1506 as his military commander. (For more on Cesare Borgia, see "The Siege of Viana" later in this chapter.)

◄ RODRIGO BORGIA (POPE ALEXANDER VI)

Rodrigo Borgia was skilled, ambitious, and a generally corrupt politician. He amassed great wealth as Vatican vice chancellor, then outmaneuvered powerful foes in the College of Cardinals to become Pope Alexander VI in 1492. As pope, Alexander had a virtual harem of mistresses; he was the first pontiff in history to acknowledge his illegitimate children as offspring, and openly treated them as such. In fact, he was accused of nepotism, and for good reason: He appointed one son, Giovanni, as commander of the Papal Army, and another son, Cesare, as a cardinal. He also carefully steered his sons and his daughter, Lucrezia, into arranged marriages that built powerful alliances with other influential families in Spain and Italy. His death in 1503 triggered more controversy and intrigue—many believe the cause to be malaria, but others suspect poison.

THE BORGIA FAMILY

The Borgia family was a powerhouse in Renaissance Italy, with a fortune built on (among other things) papal power and control of the Catholic Church's wealth.

Due to Rodrigo and Cesare's exploits and the rumors surrounding Lucrezia, the family has earned a reputation for murder and unscrupulous morals. They often used the wealth and power of the Catholic Church to further their own ends. However, their dynasty was not to last past the 1500s.

A Glass of Wine with Caesar Borgia by John Collier

LUCREZIA BORGIA ▶

Lucrezia Borgia, illegitimate daughter of Rodrigo Borgia (Pope Alexander VI) and sister of Cesare Borgia, was a woman with a cold, ruthless streak who was born into a powerful family. Without a doubt, Lucrezia participated actively in Borgia family intrigue, including a string of marriages solely for political advantage. But historical evidence suggests a strong but tragic character—a woman who had little choice but to connive to survive. Rumors of incestuous relationships with her father or brother Cesare (as depicted in the game) have never been proven (it was her first husband who made the accusation). One other interesting historical rumor, never confirmed: Lucrezia Borgia wore a hollow ring that she used regularly to poison drinks!

◀ CATERINA SFORZA

Like Lucrezia Borgia, Caterina Sforza was born illegitimately into a powerful Italian family—in Caterina's case, the Sforzas of Milan. Raised in the Milanese court, she was a refined, well-educated woman who was nonetheless quite capable of taking forceful action to protect her interests. For years she was the Countess of Forlì, a small but strategically located city-state in northeastern Italy. Her first husband, Girolamo Riario, was killed in a plot led by the rival Orsi family, and the scene in *Assassin's Creed: Brotherhood* where she dares the Orsis to kill her children by shouting, "I have the instrument to make more!" is a piece of actual history. The countess eventually defeated the Orsis and became the Regent of Forlì, ruling in the name of her son. (For more on Caterina Sforza, see "The Battle of Forlì" later in this chapter.)

FLORENCE

This longtime capital of the Italian region of Tuscany is widely considered the birthplace of the Renaissance. At the time, Florence was one of the largest and wealthiest cities in Europe. But its riches and power were not well distributed—a small elite controlled the Florentine coffers and tended to rule with a ruthless hand. Behind the scenes, powerful families like the Medici clan ran the show, and the great Tuscan city-state was often awash in a dark swirl of political intrigue. But Florence also became a cradle of enlightened thought, and provided generous patronage to many renowned artists and thinkers.

ABOVE: The bell tower of the Duomo is the highest location in *Assassin's Creed II*, and even then it had to be scaled down for the game.

RIGHT: A rejected idea for how to build the Duomo's famous dome included using dirt packed with coins as scaffolding. The citizens would then take the money and clear away the dirt after the project was finished.

Due to various Catholic traditions that involved wearing masks, Venetians could spend October through March in disguise until the 18th century when the Carnival was outlawed.

VENICE

Venice was one of the great city-states of Italy during the Renaissance, and a strong rival of Florence. With a population of 180,000, Venice was second in size only to Paris in Europe, and was very likely the wealthiest city-state in the world at that time. The Republic of Venice was well governed, well defended, and quite beautiful by all accounts. Its power and wealth were based on its strategic location at the head of the Adriatic Sea, giving it control of maritime trade between Europe and the Near East. In 1500, its navy was one of the most powerful forces in the world. But its army's crushing defeat at the Battle of Agnadello in 1509 marked the end of Venetian expansion in Italy and elsewhere.

Read more about influential Venetian brothers Agostino and Marco Barbarigo on page 32.

This spectacular structure is the cathedral of the Roman Catholic Archdiocese of Venice. Connected to the adjacent Doge's Palace, the basilica was such a symbol of opulence and power that it was often referred to as the Chiesa d'Oro, "Church of Gold."

During the Renaissance, public executions were carried out in the Piazza San Marco.

ROME

Rome's history spans more than two-and-a-half millennia and is generally regarded, along with ancient Greece, as a birthplace of Western civilization, as well as the first great metropolis in human history. After the dizzying heights of the Roman Republic and Empire—eras in which Rome dominated the known world—the city's influence declined for centuries through the Middle Ages, as waves of Asian and Germanic tribes swept back and forth across the continent. But Rome regained a measure of regional influence as the Catholic papacy expanded and consolidated the Church's vast holdings and wealth. The city was, along with Florence, a major center of the Italian Renaissance, in large part because of the powerful Catholic popes who controlled Rome's political, economic, and cultural interests.

LEFT: Often stretching for miles, the aqueducts were built as a series of arches to save materials.

BELOW: The Colosseum was abandoned for a time during the sixth century. It has been damaged by earthquakes and lightning, and portions of it were even used in the construction of other buildings.

VATICAN CITY

Medieval popes were not only spiritual leaders but also political rulers—enforcing laws and treaties, conducting diplomacy, extracting income, and even making war. Vatican City was (and still is) a walled enclave within the city of Rome, housing the headquarters of the Roman Catholic Church. In the fifteenth century, it was also the seat of power for the Papal States, the lands owned or controlled by the Church. During the Italian Renaissance, various popes used the Church's vast wealth for crass political purposes. But they also became leading patrons of the arts. As a result, Vatican City contains some of the most celebrated works in the history of art—e.g., the Apostolic Palace with its magnificent Sistine Chapel, and the Raphael Rooms in the papal apartments. These spaces feature grand fresco sequences by Michelangelo and Raphael, commissioned by Pope Julius II—works that are considered the quintessence of the High Renaissance in Rome.

CASTEL SANT'ANGELO

Originally built by the Roman Emperor Hadrian in the second century AD as a mausoleum for his family, this massive cylindrical building on the bank of Rome's Tiber River was transformed in the fourteenth century from an oversized tomb into a defensive fortress for the Vatican. Named for the archangel Michael, Castel Sant'Angelo was nearly impregnable, serving as a refuge for popes during bad times, such as the Sack of Rome in 1527. The Papal States also used the castle's lower compartments as a maximum-security prison, with executions performed in a small inner courtyard. Caterina Sforza was held here for more than a year, accused of attempting to poison Pope Alexander VI.

In *Assassin's Creed II*, Ezio travels to San Gimignano to infiltrate a Templar meeting between Grand Master Rodrigo Borgia and the Pazzi family.

SAN GIMIGNANO

This fortified township built atop a Tuscan ridge featured a central fortress and a set of remarkable watchtowers that created a unique and imposing skyline for such a small settlement. San Gimignano was a popular stop for Catholic pilgrims traveling from France to Rome. But factional fighting and family rivalries led to the construction of the lofty "tower houses." The various families kept building towers, dozens of them, higher and higher, trying to outdo each other—some more than two hundred feet tall!

MONTERIGGIONI

Monteriggioni is a walled town built on a hillock overlooking the Via Cassia, an important road running northwest from Rome up the Italian peninsula. The lords of nearby Siena originally built Monteriggioni in 1213 as a strategically placed defensive fortification in their wars with Florence. Over more than three hundred years, its walls and turrets withstood numerous attacks from Florentine armies as well as other parties looking for a commanding position in the region.

THE PAZZI CONSPIRACY

In *Assassin's Creed II*, a central story line revolves around a plot by the Pazzi family to assassinate Lorenzo the Magnificent, scion of the Medici family and de facto ruler of the Florentine Republic. In real life, the Pazzis and their allies—including Pope Sixtus IV and the archbishop of Pisa, Francesco Salviati—did indeed conspire to remove the Medici clan from power. A group of conspirators plotted to assassinate Lorenzo and his brother Giuliano de' Medici. On April 26, 1478, Easter Sunday, they carried out the attack during Mass inside the Duomo, the cathedral of Florence.

Giuliano was stabbed to death in front of ten thousand church attendees, but a wounded Lorenzo managed to escape into the cathedral's locked sacristy. The coup attempt failed, and dozens of the conspirators were eventually hunted down, captured, and hanged—including the archbishop. (Pope Sixtus managed to stay above the fray.)

ABOVE: A commemorative medal from 1478 showing the assassination of Giuliano de' Medici.

LEFT: Jacopo de' Pazzi

THE BONFIRES OF THE VANITIES

By 1497, the common folk of Florence had seen enough of the extravagance, corruption, and brazen decadence of the wealthy ruling class. Spurred on by radical reformist clergy like the Catholic monk and preacher Savonarola (see "Girolamo Savonarola" in this chapter), a movement spread across Florence denouncing the social excesses of the Florentine rich. During Mardis Gras on February 7, 1497, mobs of commoners took to the streets. Anything considered "luxury goods"—books, paintings and other works of art . . . even cosmetics, dresses, musical instruments, and playing cards—were seen as vessels of sin and burned in what were called "bonfires of the vanities."

THE BATTLE OF FORLÌ

Ruled by Caterina Sforza, Forlì was a prominent city-state in the Romagna region of northern Italy. Sforza's knowledge of military matters was extensive—in fact, she trained Forlì's militia herself. After directing a successful defense of the city against a Venetian army, she gained a new nickname: *La Tigre* (The Tiger). But in January of 1500, Forlì fell in a fierce, bloody battle to the papal armies led by Cesare Borgia, and Sforza became his prisoner. She was eventually imprisoned at Castel Sant'Angelo, where Borgia's father, Pope Alexander VI, accused her of attempts to poison him, but the trial ended inconclusively. When Alexander VI died and Borgia lost power soon after, Sforza tried to regain the family's domain in Forlì, but the new pope ultimately denied her plea.

ABOVE: Caterina Sforza, dressed in armor, rode out to meet Cesare Borgia on the field of battle.

RIGHT: Although initially barred entrance from the Forlì fortress, Caterina was able to murder the castle's keeper and capture it for herself.

In *Assassin's Creed: Brotherhood*, Ezio finally kills Cesare in Viana after a pursuit that lasted four years.

THE SIEGE OF VIANA

In 1507, King John III of Navarre put Cesare Borgia, his exiled brother-in-law, in command of his ten-thousand-man army and sent him to capture a castle in Viana, Spain. Cesare had recently escaped the infamous Castle of La Mota prison by climbing down a 130-foot tower using a rope—a great comedown for the man who had once been Captain General of the Papal Army and the most powerful lord in northern Italy. During the Siege of Viana, a party of enemy knights escaped in a rainstorm. Borgia instinctively gave chase, assuming that his men would follow. They didn't. When the knights realized that only one man was in pursuit, they turned on him. The results were not good for Borgia, who ended up on the wrong end of a spear.

Read more about Cesare Borgia on page 33.

CHAPTER 3

THE OTTOMAN EMPIRE, SIXTEENTH CENTURY

■

Assassin's Creed: Revelations features the return of Ezio Auditore da Firenze, placing him in both Masyaf and Constantinople during the years 1511 and 1512. But in the course of the story, Ezio accesses the memories of the protagonist from the original *Assassin's Creed,* Altaïr Ibn-La'Ahad. In those memories, Altaïr explores Masyaf back in the twelfth and thirteenth century. We've already looked at that locale, so we'll focus this chapter's attention on Ezio's engagements in the Ottoman Empire.

EZIO IN ASSASSIN'S CREED REVELATIONS

It is the year 1511, and Ezio, now in his mid-fifties, travels to the Assassin fortress of Masyaf in search of Altaïr's secret library. Older and wiser, Ezio's character has gained a deep level of sophistication and self-confidence. His focus and dedication allow him to play a central role in the final days of Bayezid II's reign in Constantinople.

HISTORICAL OVERVIEW

The Ottoman Empire, a composite of Turkish tribes based in Asia Minor, had become a major world power by 1511. At the time, the empire included all of present-day Turkey and many of the territories east of the Adriatic Sea, stretching from southeastern Europe around the Black Sea. Much of this conquest occurred during the reign of Sultan Mehmed II (1451–81), who conquered Constantinople in 1453 at the age of twenty-one and, for the next thirty years, never stopped expanding and reshaping the empire. From 1481 to 1512, Mehmed's son Bayezid II ruled over a period of consolidation and relative peace, quashing a few minor rebellions and developing administrative systems to govern the sprawling, diverse state.

THE WAR OF SUCCESSION

By 1509, however, powerful groups within Bayezid's ruling coalition—in particular, the Janissaries, the sultan's elite military corps—wanted a more activist, militant leadership. This led to a bloody three-year struggle between Bayezid's sons Ahmet and Selim. Ahmet was the oldest son and Bayezid's first choice—he was well liked in the sultan's court and the general populace, and he was a capable governor. Unfortunately for Ahmet, the Janissaries regarded him as a weak military leader, and preferred the more pitiless tactics and leadership of Selim. In 1512, the Janissary corps forced Bayezid to abdicate in favor of Selim, who quickly and ruthlessly consolidated power.

Under the sultanates of Selim I and then his son Suleiman I (known as "Suleiman the Magnificent"), Ottoman control would spread across much of the present-day Middle East, extending all the way across Egypt and the northern coast of Africa nearly to the Atlantic.

Concept art of the Hagia Sophia in Constantinople. During the reign of Suleiman, minarets and exterior buttresses were added to the church's perimeter.

HISTORICAL CHARACTERS

◄ SEHZADE AHMET

This Ottoman crown prince ("Sehzade" is "prince" in Turkish) was the oldest son of Sultan Bayezid II, and his father's chosen heir. In the early days of the struggle with his younger brother Selim for the right to succeed Bayezid as sultan, Ahmet seemed to have the upper hand. When his father's army defeated an insurrection by Selim's forces in 1511, Ahmet's path to the Ottoman throne looked clear. Unfortunately, his own soldiers considered him weak. When Selim picked up the support of the powerful Janissaries, the issue was decided. In April of 1513, Ahmet and his remaining troops fought the new sultan's army in Bursa province. Selim won easily, and Ahmet was executed.

BAYEZID II

Although he was known as "Bayezid the Just" for his efforts to ensure a fairer, less violent internal politics in the empire, the sultan was no stranger to ugly struggles for the right of succession. This son of the great military leader Mehmed II had to fight hard against his brother Cem in order to attain the Ottoman sultanate. So when his own sons threatened civil war over who would succeed him, Bayezid tried to head it off by declaring support for his oldest son and natural heir, Ahmet. His youngest, Selim, was not pleased. After three years of nasty intrafamily conflict, Selim seized the upper hand. Forced to abdicate his throne, Bayezid traveled to Dimetoka, the city of his birth, to retire . . . but never quite made it. He died en route, most likely from poisoning.

SELIM ▶

The youngest son of Bayezid II was the most ambitious and ruthless of the sultan's offspring. Selim was a favorite of the Janissary corps because he shared his grandfather Mehmed's militant thirst for conquest. Selim's ruthless approach to power extended to family matters as well. After dethroning his father, Selim directed a purge of all relatives who could lay claim to the throne. His emissaries assassinated his two brothers, all seven of their sons . . . and four of Selim's own five sons! This left only his favored son, Suleiman, alive as heir.

◀ SULEIMAN

In 1512, Suleiman became the crown prince and undisputed heir to the Ottoman throne. He went on to succeed his father just eight years later, at age twenty-six, after Selim I's 1520 death. Although a young man, Suleiman had been educated at the finest palace schools in Constantinople, and by age twenty he'd already served as a viceroy (governor) in three cities. He proved to be one of the more capable rulers in history, and was widely known as Suleiman the Magnificent. He eventually became the longest-reigning Ottoman sultan, ruling for forty-six years. Those years would prove to be the historical high point of the empire's military, economic, and political power.

Piri Reis's map of America is one of the oldest in existence

PIRI REIS

Ahmed Muhiddin Piri was the famed Ottoman naval
commander, geographer, and cartographer who wrote the
Kitab-ı Bahriye, a renowned treatise on navigation. Its final
edition included more than 250 charts of the cities and ports
of the Mediterranean that are remarkably accurate for their
time. The term *reis* is a Turkish military rank that translates
as "admiral"—hence he was referred to as Piri Reis. He took
part in many important sea battles, serving as a commander
in the Ottoman Navy until he was almost ninety years old.
But Piri is best known for his remarkable "Piri Reis map,"
a world map first compiled in 1513, then redrawn in 1528,
that included territories in the New World that had been
discovered only recently by Christopher Columbus.

Artwork of Piri Reis's world map created for *Assassin's
Creed: Revelations.*

◄ MANUEL PALAIOLOGOS

Manuel Palaiologos was the son of Thomas Palaiologos, heir to the Byzantine throne. After the Ottomans conquered Constantinople in 1453, Thomas took his family, including Manuel, into exile in Rome. After his father died, Manuel Palaiologos remained in Rome for a while. But once he reached adulthood, Palaiologos shocked the Vatican by returning to Constantinople and placing himself at the mercy of the Ottoman sultan, Mehmed II, who had conquered the city. In exchange for giving up all rights to the Byzantine Imperial throne, Palaiologos was granted an estate and a generous pension. He died at age fifty-seven in 1512, just as the Ottoman civil war between the sons of Bayezid II, Ahmet and Selim, drew to a lethal conclusion.

NICCOLÒ POLO ►

Although Niccolò Polo (right) is probably best known as the father of the famed traveler Marco Polo, he was a great traveler in his own right. The Polos were a family of wealthy merchants in Venice, and as part of his mercantile business, Niccolò journeyed with his brother Maffeo (left) throughout Asia to find trading partners. On their first trip, Niccolò and Maffeo established a trading post in Constantinople during the 1250s and lived there for several years, becoming very familiar with the city. After fifteen years, the Polo brothers returned home, and then Marco joined them on their next Asian trip—an epic journey that lasted twenty-four years!

KEY LOCATIONS, LANDMARKS, AND EVENTS

CONSTANTINOPLE IN 1511

For almost an entire millennium, the Byzantine Empire was the single most powerful economic and political force in Europe. Its capital, Constantinople, was the continent's largest and richest city for centuries, commanding the trade routes between East and West. But by the middle of the fifteenth century, the empire and its capital had suffered serious decline. The rise and spread of the Ottoman Empire hemmed in the Byzantine city, leaving it isolated. Finally, in May of 1453, Constantinople fell to the Ottoman army of Sultan Mehmed II, marking the end of the Byzantine Empire. The city became the new Ottoman capital, and Mehmed instituted the vigorous repair, renovation, and upgrade of buildings and utilities. By 1511, Constantinople had been much restored, transformed into a magnificent multicultural city.

ABOVE: Art of Constantinople's harbor and walls

OPPOSITE: Constantinople was slightly smaller than Rome; its densely populated streets and shops created the sense of a maze in the game.

DERINKUYU

Derinkuyu was a remarkable multilevel underground city, one of several located in the region of Cappadocia in Central Anatolia, a province of the Ottoman Empire. Some of the lower chambers of this subterranean complex were excavated at a depth of two hundred feet. The city was large enough to hold as many as twenty thousand inhabitants, with storage rooms holding months of supplies, stables for livestock, dining rooms, a winery, oil presses, a huge vaulted chamber used as a school, and a cruciform church on the lowest level (the fifth floor underground). Little is known of the city's history, but it appears to have been used by Cappadocian Greek locals as a refuge from Ottoman invaders in the fifteenth and sixteenth centuries.

OPPOSITE: The underground city in the game was based both on the real Derinkuyu and the ancient city of Petra.

THE JANISSARIES

Formed in 1383, this elite corps of Ottoman infantry served as the Sultan's household troops and personal bodyguards for five centuries. Interestingly, Janissary units were composed entirely of war captives and slaves. In many cases the captives were peasant youth, kidnapped and conscripted into the corps. Trained for years under tough conditions and the strictest rules of behavior, Janissaries were highly disciplined soldiers, and greatly feared. They were often rewarded with spoils of battle, so they had a vested interest in maintaining a culture of conquest. In 1512, this fact led to the corps' support of Selim in his claim to the sultanate over his less warlike brother Ahmet.

Artwork of a Turkish yatagan sword, the signature weapon of the Janissaries

CHAPTER 4

THE GOLDEN AGE OF PIRACY

Set in the early 1700s, *Assassin's Creed IV: Black Flag* features the fictional Edward Kenway, a Welsh privateer who chooses to embrace a life of piracy in the Caribbean. Here we jump ahead in the game series to keep our historical review in chronological order—in a real-life timeline, the events of *Assassin's Creed IV* are actually set before those of *Assassin's Creed III*.

EDWARD KENWAY

During the War of Spanish Succession, the British government commissioned privateers, armed ships legally allowed to attack and loot enemy merchant vessels, in an attempt to weaken Spain's formidable naval forces. It is in these times that Edward Kenway decides to make his fortune by joining the Royal Navy as a privateer. However, the war soon ends, and Edward finds himself on the wrong side of the law as a pirate. Ever in pursuit of fame and wealth, he becomes entangled in the dealings of the Assassins and Templars in the West Indies.

HISTORICAL OVERVIEW

Concept art of the warfare tactic of broadsiding. Two ships would align and then open fire, destroying lower decks and vital rigging.

The Golden Age of Piracy lasted roughly from 1700 to 1725, during a period when the American Colonial shipping trade was beginning to boom. Hundreds of commercial ships laden with valuable goods and treasure sailed across the Atlantic every month. These vessels became easy prey for maritime raiders based in the Caribbean and along the North American seaboard.

PRIVATEERING AND PIRACY

During wartime in the seventeenth and eighteenth centuries, governments in Europe bestowed "letters of marque" on private ship owners, giving them full authority to attack and plunder enemy vessels. This practice was called "privateering." Ambitious citizens with first-rate boats and crews could wreak havoc on enemy shipping lanes, making a tidy profit while serving the national interest. Privateers gave countries a way to mobilize armed fleets into a self-funding paramilitary navy.

Privateers, then, were essentially pirates with legal authority to plunder. In practice, the line between the two grew increasingly blurry. Most notorious pirates of the Golden Age started their careers as privateers. Some pirates even claimed to be doing "the king's work" as they preyed upon merchant shipping on the high seas. Privateer and pirate crews were often filled with remarkably skilled sailors and soldiers. The reason: Naval seamen typically earned low wages, whereas every pirate earned a share of the booty. The more plunder, the more pay!

THE REPUBLIC OF PIRATES

In 1696, the pirate Henry Avery sailed into the harbor at Nassau in the Bahamas with shiploads of stolen loot. He bribed the governor into making Nassau a safe refuge for privateers—in essence, a protected pirate base. By 1706, many of the island's settlers had abandoned the colony, leaving it in a lawless state. Thus pirates led by the pirate captain Benjamin Hornigold organized Nassau into a commune of sorts, with informal leaders and even a code of conduct. As word got out, English privateers flocked to Nassau to join the so-called Republic of Pirates. Outlaw luminaries like Blackbeard, Charles Vane, Calico Jack, Anne Bonny, Mary Read, and others helped turn Nassau into a legendary locale filled with infamous exploits.

Seeking to put an end to the enterprise, the British officially declared the Bahamas a crown colony in 1718, appointed Woodes Rogers governor, and sent him to reclaim the settlement. (See "Woodes Rogers" later in this chapter.) Within two years Rogers had greatly reduced the pirate presence on the islands—the beginning of the end for the Golden Age of Piracy.

PIRATE CUTLASS

When a pirate boarded a ship for capture, he (or she) usually carried a short slashing sword called a "cutlass" for hand-to-hand combat in the tight quarters of a ship's deck. The cutlass was a very common naval weapon.

Roles aboard a pirate ship include the boatswain, the crewman in charge of supplies and ship inspection; the rigger, who furled and released the sails; and the quartermaster, second in command to the captain.

HISTORICAL CHARACTERS

Iconic artwork of Blackbeard aboard the *Queen Anne's Revenge*

◄ EDWARD "BLACKBEARD" THATCH

Edward Thatch started his career as a privateer but soon "went pirate," joining the crew of Benjamin Hornigold in 1716. Within a year Thatch was captaining his own ship and had become the infamous Blackbeard, the pirate demon who terrorized the eastern seaboard of the American colonies. He worked the Caribbean as well, preying on shipping lanes in his famous 200-ton frigate, the *Queen Anne's Revenge*. Thatch's huge, imposing presence—he threaded lit fuses through his wild beard and hair—would scare victims into giving up their loot without a fight. Interestingly, despite his image, he never murdered or even harmed his captives. In his final battle, Blackbeard boarded a British naval sloop but found his crew outnumbered. He fought furiously, reportedly taking five gunshots and twenty cutlass wounds without slowing until a British sailor snuck up and whacked off his head.

◀ BARTHOLOMEW ROBERTS

In terms of raw numbers, Bartholomew Roberts was the most successful pirate of the Golden Age. His crews plundered a whopping four hundred ships between 1719 and 1722! His life of piracy began when the Welsh pirate captain Howell Davis captured his merchant vessel and forcibly conscripted Roberts into his crew. The new recruit gained so much respect that when Davis was killed in action not long afterward, the crew named Roberts their new captain! In 1721, he seized a massive, forty-cannon frigate that he renamed *Royal Fortune*. It became one of the most formidable pirate flagships ever, rivaling even Blackbeard's vaunted *Queen Anne's Revenge* for power and speed. Many historians feel that Roberts' dramatic death while fighting Royal Navy warships in 1722 marks the end of the Golden Age of Piracy. (One last note: His famous nickname—"Black Bart"—was actually never used in his lifetime.)

BENJAMIN HORNIGOLD ▶

A founder of the infamous Republic of Pirates in Nassau, Hornigold began his career as a West Indies privateer. In the early years, his great thirty-gun sloop was the most powerful ship in the region; in addition, Hornigold's second-in-command was none other than Edward "Blackbeard" Thatch. Soon he'd increased his pirate flotilla to five ships and 350 sailors. But within a year Hornigold surprised his pirate peers by seeking the king's pardon from Woodes Rogers, the new governor of the Bahamas. He was commissioned as a pirate hunter and spent eighteen months hunting down old friends until he was killed in a shipwreck during the hurricane season of 1719.

◄ CHARLES VANE

Another feared pirate who was based in Nassau, Vane preyed with impunity on both French and English shipping from 1716 to 1719. His flagship, a brigantine called the *Ranger*, became a starting point for a number of other famed pirate captains, including "Calico Jack" Rackham and Edward England, each serving as Vane's quartermaster for a time. Known for cruel treatment of his captives, Vane so terrorized the Bahaman seas that commercial shipping ground to a near halt in 1718. But after a shipwreck, Vane was marooned on an island for weeks, and then "rescued" by a ship that took him straight to a Jamaican jail. Like many of his fellow pirates, he ended up hanged at Gallows Point in Port Royal.

STEDE BONNET ►

Often called "The Gentleman Pirate" in reference to the profitable sugar plantation he inherited in Barbados, Bonnet was nonetheless a restless adventurer who turned to piracy out of boredom. In 1717, despite his lack of sailing knowledge, he bought a 60-ton sloop with six cannons and named it *Revenge*. In Nassau's notorious den of pirates, he met Edward "Blackbeard" Thatch, who mentored him in captaincy. While commanding the *Revenge* for Bonnet, Blackbeard captured a huge, 200-ton frigate that he turned into his famous flagship, the *Queen Anne's Revenge*. Bonnet eventually retook command of his own ship and began raiding along the East Coast. After a fierce battle at the mouth of Cape Fear River in North Carolina, Bonnet was captured by pirate hunters. Not even his gentleman's reputation could save him—like so many other pirates of the Golden Age, he was tried and hanged.

JOHN "CALICO JACK" RACKHAM ▶

Calico Jack began his career as quartermaster on Charles Vane's two-masted *Ranger* in 1718, operating out of the pirate haven in Nassau. On a raid near New York, they ran into a powerful French man-of-war—a heavily armed warship twice the size of the *Ranger*. Vane ordered an immediate retreat, but Rackham protested, wanting to turn back and fight. Vane refused to reconsider his order, and the *Ranger* escaped the man-of-war. But the next day, the crew decided to remove Vane for cowardice, and made Calico Jack the new captain!

◀ ANNE BONNY

The Irishwoman Anne McCormac married a sailor named James Bonny, and somehow they ended up in Nassau. There, she promptly left her husband for Calico Jack Rackham. Joined by another partner, Mary Read, they sailed the islands, raiding numerous vessels. Anne participated fully in combat and was well respected by the other pirates. But in 1720, a pirate hunter launched a surprise attack and captured the entire crew. Most were tried and hanged, including Calico Jack, but Anne Bonny and Mary Read pleaded for stays of execution because both were pregnant. Read died during childbirth. No record exists of Bonny's fate. Historians suggest that her father, a wealthy merchant in the Carolinas, simply bought her freedom. Some clues indicate that Anne returned home, married a Virginian, bore eight children, and lived into her eighties!

WOODES ROGERS ▶

Rogers started as a merchant sailor, inheriting his father's shipping business at age twenty-seven. Looking for trade routes, he outfitted two frigates and set sail. His first voyage lasted three years, and he became the first English sailor to circumnavigate the globe and return with all ships intact. (He also rescued a seaman named Selkirk who was marooned alone on a Pacific island—the inspiration for Daniel Defoe's classic novel *Robinson Crusoe*.) In 1718, Rogers led a force to the Bahamas, where King George I had appointed him governor to enforce British rule. Rogers drove pirates from the colony and added Benjamin Hornigold to his employ as a pirate hunter. Rogers was appointed to a second term as governor in 1729. But suffering from poor health, he died in Nassau three years later.

KEY LOCATIONS AND LANDMARKS

Located along the sailing routes for treasures from the New World, Havana was a natural target for pirates.

HAVANA (CUBA)

Capital of Cuba and trading center of the Caribbean, Havana was a flourishing colony port for the Spanish Crown in the early 1700s. The city had expanded greatly in the previous century, adding great structures that included three castle forts and several defensive towers guarding waterway entrances. Great merchant fleets would gather in Havana Bay to rendezvous with Spain's armada of warships for protection against pirates on the long voyage back to Europe. Within a few years, Havana had grown to one of the largest cities in the Americas, bigger than New York and Boston. In fact, Spain officially designated Havana as "Key to the New World."

Havana Cathedral was actually built after Edward Kenway's time, but was included in the game as a recognizable landmark.

During its short two-year stint, Blackbeard's legendary flagship was the most feared vessel on the high seas. Formerly a French slaving ship, the massive frigate with its blistering forty-cannon battery could engage even a frontline Royal Navy warship, yet it was fast enough to escape easily when facing superior numbers. With the fearsome Blackbeard on the bridge and his skilled, veteran crew on deck and gunnery, the *Queen Anne's Revenge* ruled the Atlantic shipping lanes. In 1718, Blackbeard used the great ship and a flotilla of support vessels to blockade the entire port of Charleston, South Carolina, withdrawing only after extracting a ransom of medical supplies. But soon after, the *Queen Anne's Revenge* hit a sandbar off the North Carolina coast, damaging it beyond repair. The frigate had to be scuttled—that is, deliberately sunk—after the transfer of its supplies to other ships in his flotilla.

An overhead rendering of the island created for *Assassin's Creed IV: Black Flag*.

NASSAU (BAHAMAS)

Nassau was the site of a colonial settlement on New Providence Island in the Bahamas, a chain of about seven hundred islands in the Atlantic Ocean, southeast of Florida. For several years after 1703, Nassau and the surrounding islands became so sparsely populated that it had no governor, nor any organized government to speak of. By 1713 the Bahamas had turned into a safe haven for privateers and pirates. (See "The Republic of Pirates" in this chapter.)

In addition to its thriving port, Kingston was also the location of large sugar plantations.

KINGSTON (JAMAICA)

In 1692, after a massive earthquake destroyed Port Royal in Jamaica—a vibrant center of shipping commerce (and piracy) in the Caribbean at the time—that city's survivors moved to the sleepy agricultural villa of Kingston on the southeast coast of the island. By 1716, Kingston had exploded in size, dominating trade in not just Jamaica but the entire British West Indies. Inland sugarcane plantations fueled much of the growth; slave traders based in Kingston made a fortune supplying forced labor for Jamaica's sugar boom. After the War of the Spanish Succession ended, Kingston's population began to swell even more, as unemployed sailors and privateers drifted into town looking for work. They found "work" in the crews forming in the city, which had inherited some of Port Royal's unsavory reputation as a haven for smugglers, pirates, and prostitutes.

Slaver and plantation owner Laurens Prins's mansion, which is based on actual manor houses from that period.

CHAPTER 5

THE SEVEN YEARS' WAR

Assassin's Creed: Rogue features a Templar protagonist, Shay Patrick Cormac. Shay starts as a member of the Assassin Brotherhood but soon defects to the other side. Set in the North Atlantic region of North America, it introduces Cormac to a string of Colonial American figures. The game takes place just one year after the final events of *Assassin's Creed IV: Black Flag*. Its story also serves as a prequel for *Assassin's Creed III* and connects to *Assassin's Creed Unity* as well.

SHAY CORMAC

At the start of *Assassin's Creed: Rogue,* Shay Patrick Cormac is a member of the Brotherhood of Assassins in Colonial America. Already questioning the Assassin's methods when tracking down two Pieces of Eden, Shay's belief in the Creed is shattered when his discovery of a First Civilization temple in Lisbon sets off a massive earthquake, which kills thousands. He was inducted into the Templar Order and began working with Grand Master Haytham Kenway to destroy the Colonial Assassin Brotherhood in the midst of the Seven Years' War.

HISTORICAL OVERVIEW

The Seven Years' War raged across Europe and other parts of the world from 1756 to 1763. The conflict ultimately involved almost every great power of the era. In fact, the war was so widespread that it acquired many different names, depending on the geographic region. But its primary antagonists were France and Great Britain. Their bitter conflict actually began in 1754 on the frontier in North America, when British Colonial troops attacked French holdings in the Ohio River Valley. There, it became known as the French and Indian War.

In North America, then, the conflict played out as a struggle between the British America colonies and New France, joined by its Native American allies. At the war's beginning, French colonial settlers numbered just sixty thousand, whereas the British Crown colonies had a combined population of more than two million. But despite that disadvantage, the French enjoyed a string of early successes that kept the British colonials off balance, thanks to France's extensive network of Native American allies. These tribal nations were fierce, capable fighters.

Ultimately, however, the British side prevailed, and the French agreed to make significant concessions in the Treaty of Paris, signed in 1763. Everything France owned east of the Mississippi River was ceded to Great Britain.

Britain's naval prowess at the Battle of Lagos and the Battle of Quiberon Bay prevented the French from invading England and added many more colonies to England's growing empire.

HISTORICAL CHARACTERS

◄ BENJAMIN FRANKLIN

As the Seven Years' War geared up in North America, Franklin was an assembly-man in Pennsylvania. Beyond his never-ending string of inventions and scientific experiments with electricity and lightning rods, Franklin found time to establish a college that eventually became the University of Pennsylvania—a school that would produce many of the so-called Founding Fathers of the United States, who later crafted the Declaration of Independence. During the Seven Years' War, Franklin traveled to London and emerged as the leading spokesman for American Colonial interests, often arguing the American case in the British House of Commons against excessive taxes like the Stamp Act or other "colonial exploitation."

LAWRENCE WASHINGTON ►

Lawrence Washington was George Washington's beloved older half brother. When their father died of a sudden illness, George was just eleven years old. Lawrence, who was twenty-five, became George's surrogate father and role model. He inherited a family property that he named Mount Vernon; it would eventually pass on to George and become one of the most venerated estates in American history. Lawrence was a member of the Colonial legislature and a well-respected man. Unfortunately, he contracted tuberculosis and died at Mount Vernon in 1752.

◄ GEORGE WASHINGTON

George Washington, a young officer in the Virginia militia, happened to participate in events that triggered the start of the French and Indian War, which in turn sparked the global Seven Years' War. He was involved in the first skirmishes related to the provocative French construction of Fort Duquesne on the Ohio River. (Control of the Ohio River Valley was a highly charged issue between the French and British Colonial authorities.) After the skirmishes, Washington became the senior American aide to General Edward Braddock, who led a British expedition to expel the French from the valley. (For more on this, see our next chapter, "The American Revolution.")

SIR WILLIAM JOHNSON (FIRST BARONET) ▶

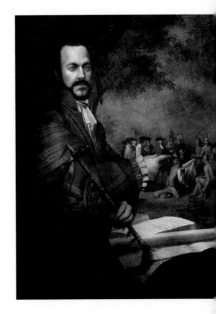

As a young man, William Johnson lived on an estate in the Province of New York. His land was surrounded by villages of the Kanien'kehá:ka people (also known as the "Mohawk"), one of the Six Nations of the Iroquois League. Because Johnson learned the tribe's language and customs, he was named Indian commissioner for the Province of New York in 1750. As war began to spread across the North American theater, Johnson was commissioned as a major general in command of all Iroquois and Colonial militia forces. In 1755, he led his troops in a much-needed victory at the Battle of Lake George, for which King George made him a baronet. A year later, Johnson became the British superintendent of Indian affairs for the northern colonies, maintaining the Crown's military partnership with the Iroquois confederacy and other northern tribes.

◀ LOUIS-JOSEPH GAULTIER, CHEVALIER DE LA VÉRENDRYE

Born into a family of French Canadian fur traders in New France, Louis-Joseph Gaultier took up the family business at a young age. Along with his father and brothers, he extended the fur trade west of Lake Superior and became the first European traveler to reach the Rocky Mountains via the Great Plains. He assisted in building several major French forts on the frontier, and in 1756, Gaultier was appointed commandant overseeing all outposts in the west. However, he was so deeply involved in the military concerns of the Seven Years' War that he never left the east. Once Quebec fell to the British, he set sail for France. But en route his ship, the *Auguste*, sank off the coast of Cape Breton in November of 1760.

GEORGE MONRO ▶

Monro was a lifelong soldier in the British Army, serving without much fanfare for almost forty years. By 1757, he had risen to the rank of lieutenant colonel and been sent to the Americas. That spring, Monro was assigned to Fort William Henry, an isolated outpost in upstate New York. A large French force soon attacked, and the lieutenant colonel led a spirited defense. But his garrison was greatly outnumbered, and he surrendered. (For more on the terrible event, see "The Siege of Fort William Henry" in this chapter.) Afterward, Monro returned to Albany, New York, where he died just three months later of "apoplexy"—a term in those days that meant sudden death, as by a stroke or heart attack. It was said that he died of anguish over the events at Fort William Henry.

KEY LOCATIONS, LANDMARKS, AND EVENTS

Artwork depicting a bleak New York road during winter

NEW YORK CITY

At the time of the Seven Years' War, New York was already a cosmopolitan city. As a strategically important trading center, it was bustling with commercial activity, shipbuilding, and maritime trade. Reports at the time spoke of proud, well-dressed, lively citizens with a "fresh outlook" that included freedom of worship, and—after a 1735 libel trial that guaranteed freedom of the press—an openly questioning attitude toward the British Colonial authorities. Thus, in many ways, the Colonial city had already thrown off the yoke of its mother country, England. During the war, New York City was the primary base for British military operations, as it would be also in the next war—the American Revolution.

Fort William Henry was a relatively small, isolated British outpost on the shore of Lake George in New York. In the spring of 1757, as hostilities between Britain and France began to flare up, Lieutenant Colonel George Monro took command of the fort's garrison of 2,500 British soldiers and Colonial militia. Soon a large force of 6,200 French soldiers and 1,800 American Indians under General Louis-Joseph de Montcalm arrived and laid siege to the fort. After three days of heavy bombardment, Monro had little choice but to negotiate terms of surrender. Montcalm agreed to allow the garrison (which included a number of women and children) to march unharmed to another British fort nearby. But as the evacuation began, the Native Americans allied with the French fell furiously on the defenseless British soldiers and civilians and began to massacre them. Dozens were killed, and hundreds more were carried off into captivity. Monro and a few others escaped, and the incident became a rallying cry for the British colonials in the war.

ABOVE RIGHT: Montcalm trying to stop Native Americans from attacking British soldiers and civilians as they leave Fort William Henry. Wood engraving by Albert Bobbett after a painting by Felix Octavius Carr Darley.

THE GREAT LISBON EARTHQUAKE OF 1755

This terrifying event occurred on November 1, 1755. First, a powerful quake with an estimated magnitude of 8.5 to 9.0 shattered Lisbon, and then three separate tsunami waves thundered through the Portuguese city, wreaking terrible destruction. Witnesses reported that the shaking lasted more than four minutes, ripping open fissures in the ground up to fifteen feet wide. Then, forty minutes later, the first tsunami wave roared ashore through the harbor and downtown, knocking down everything left standing after the temblor. Great palaces, cathedrals, libraries, and museums were lost. The quake's shock was felt throughout Europe, and gigantic waves produced by the seismic movement were recorded in England, North Africa, and as far away as Brazil. In the end, thirty thousand people were killed and about 85 percent of Lisbon's buildings were destroyed.

ASSASSIN'S CREED: LIBERATION

Set in the interim between the Seven Years' War and the American Revolution (roughly 1765 to 1777), the story of *Assassin's Creed: Liberation* depicts the exploits of Aveline de Grandpré, a French-African member of the Assassins Brotherhood operating in New Orleans and the surrounding Louisiana bayous.

AVELINE DE GRANDPRÉ

Aveline is an eighteenth-century Assassin caught between two worlds, fighting to find her true purpose. A strong defender of the slaves and others who are downtrodden or oppressed, Aveline fought for freedom during the Seven Years' War and eventually eradicated the Templar presence in New Orleans.

ABOVE: Concept art of the construction of Saint Louis Cathedral in Jackson Square. Note the New Orleans flag to the right.

COLONIAL NEW ORLEANS

Founded in 1718 by French colonists, the city of New Orleans was a relatively insignificant port in its early years. The city's initial residents were a colorful multiracial mix of traders, slaves, convicts, and indigents who laid the foundation of a truly unique culture. Although the port of New Orleans linked much of North America's interior regions to the rest of the world's trade via the Mississippi River system, the value of this waterway connection was not fully realized until later in the 1700s when New Orleans became a great cotton port.

In 1763, after the British victory in the Seven Years' War, all French lands west of the Mississippi River, including New Orleans, were ceded to the Spanish Empire. The local population was not pleased and even revolted unsuccessfully against Spanish rule in 1768. Spain managed to maintain control of the city for forty years. During the American Revolution, New Orleans served as an important entry point for aid smuggled to the American colonial cause.

LOUISIANA VOODOO

The game makes references to "voodoo." This was a set of spiritual beliefs that came from West Africa to French Louisiana via the Atlantic slave trade in the early 1700s. Voodoo is rooted in spirit and ancestor worship and in the use of charms, amulets, and dolls for protection, healing, or curses. Knowledge of herbs and poisons was also important to voodoo practice as it developed amongst the slave population of colonial Louisiana.

CHAPTER 6

THE AMERICAN REVOLUTION

Assassin's Creed III depicts foundational events in the birth of the United States from 1754 to 1783. Many of the characters are familiar figures—George Washington, Samuel Adams, Lafayette, Paul Revere. In this installment, the modern-day protagonist Desmond Miles briefly taps into the ancestral memories of a Templar, Haytham Kenway, some years before the Revolution. But soon the perspective shifts to the memories of Kenway's son, a half-British, half-Kanien'kehá:ka (the Native American people also known as the "Mohawk" tribe) man named Ratonhnhaké:ton—who goes by the name Connor.

CONNOR

The son of Haytham Kenway and a Kanien'kehá:ka woman named Kaniehtí:io, Ratonhnhaké:ton, also known as Connor, saw his village burned and his mother killed by what he believed were Templar forces. Searching for justice and a means to protect the remaining members of his tribe, Connor convinces Mentor Achilles Davenport to train him as an Assassin. As he hunted Templars and tried to reconcile his relationship with his father, Connor would find that his goal of true freedom might be unattainable in the time of the Revolutionary War.

HISTORICAL OVERVIEW

"And above all else, men: Do not fire until you see the whites of their eyes."

—Quote attributed to Major General Israel Putnam and addressed to his American colonial troops at the Battle of Bunker Hill, June 17, 1775, that was also in *Assassin's Creed III*

The American Revolution was the military conflict in which the Thirteen Colonies of North America fought for independence from their mother country, Great Britain. By 1765, American dissenters calling themselves Patriots were formally rejecting the authority of the British Parliament to levy unreasonable taxes. Protests intensified over the next ten years, with some turning into violent confrontations like the Boston Massacre (discussed later in this chapter) and the Boston Tea Party, where Colonial protesters attacked merchant vessels and tossed chests of heavily taxed tea into the harbor. When the British responded with punitive laws, the other colonies rallied behind Massachusetts. By April 1775, fighting broke out between British Army regulars and Colonial militia groups at Lexington and Concord, the first military engagements of the Revolution.

A DECLARATION OF INDEPENDENCE

Representatives from all thirteen colonies gathered to form their own provincial congress and assemble local militias into a centralized defense force called the Continental Army. The Continental Congress handed command to General George Washington. Then, on July 4, 1776, the assembly signed the Declaration of Independence. The landmark document rejected the concept of monarchy, asserting that "all men are created equal." It also proclaimed the Thirteen Colonies to be independent states, free of British rule.

Back in Britain, Parliament began to deploy more troops to quell the rebellion. But although Great Britain was the preeminent Colonial power in 1776, it had many pressing concerns in Europe, as well as other regions worldwide. This worked in America's favor as Washington slowly (and sometimes painfully—see "Valley Forge" in this chapter) built his Continental Army into a tough, resilient fighting force. Colonial forces had time to overcome early setbacks. The British also misjudged the depth of support for the movement, seeing it as a small-scale uprising that could be quashed with a show of force.

General Washington was able to drive the British out of Boston, win small but psychologically important victories at Trenton and Princeton, and keep the enemy off balance. By the time Colonial forces surrounded and captured an entire British army at Saratoga in 1777, the tide was turning. France and Spain entered the war on the American side. With help from the French fleet, Washington managed to trap another British army, led by General Charles Cornwallis, at Yorktown, Virginia, in 1781. Stunned by news of the decisive defeat, Britain's Parliament voted to suspend military operations in North America. In 1783, the Treaty of Paris formally ended the war, and recognized the independence and sovereignty of the United States.

After the Declaration of Independence was adopted, copies were made the next day. Only twenty-six of these rare documents survive today, three of which are privately owned.

HISTORICAL CHARACTERS

◄ CHARLES LEE

A former British Army officer, Charles Lee believed so fervently in the American rebellion that he left everything he owned in England to cross the Atlantic and join the cause. A blunt, aggressive man who'd lost fingers dueling in Europe, Lee brought significant military experience to the colonies and became a major general in the Continental Army, second in rank only to George Washington. At times, he was a talented soldier who served capably. But his undisguised disdain for Washington's leadership created problems; Lee saw himself as better suited to be commander in chief. During the Battle of Monmouth in June of 1778, Lee's disorganized vanguard units fell apart. When Washington arrived, Lee engaged his commander in a heated public exchange that led to his court-martial and temporary dismissal for insubordination. Instead of repairing the rift, Lee criticized Congress for refusing to overturn the verdict and continued to openly attack Washington's character. As a result, his dismissal became permanent in 1780. He died of a fever in Philadelphia two years later.

EDWARD BRADDOCK ►

General Braddock was commander in chief of all British forces in North America at the start of the French and Indian War. In 1755, he led an ill-fated campaign against French forces based at Fort Duquesne in the Ohio River Valley. His staff included a young volunteer aide named George Washington, a Colonial officer. After crossing the Monongahela River on July 9, 1755, Braddock ran into a sizable force of French troops with Native American allies. In the ensuing battle, the general took a musket ball through the chest. Before Braddock died, he passed his military sash on to Washington, who was so moved that he kept it with him the rest of his life . . . including his term as first president of the United States.

"I, this day, declare with the utmost sincerity, I do not think myself equal to the Command I am honored with."

—Real quote from George Washington, accepting his appointment as Commander of the Continental Army, June 1775

GEORGE WASHINGTON ▶

The "father of his country" started out the American Revolution in a rough spot. As commander in chief of the Continental Army, Washington led an undertrained, poorly equipped militia against a professional army considered the most formidable fighting force in the world. Despite that, he managed to drive the British out of Boston, and then made famous winter crossings of the Delaware River to surprise British forces at Trenton and Princeton, two decisive victories for the colonies. After Washington (with the help of a French fleet and troops) surrounded and captured a major British army led by General Cornwallis at Yorktown in 1781, the British government finally began to negotiate an end to the conflict.

It was at this point that Washington made perhaps his most universally admired command decision: In the name of American republicanism, he resigned his post as commander in chief, refusing to seize the dictatorial power readily available to him. Even King George III of England, when he heard of Washington's plans, reportedly said, "If he does that, he will be the greatest man in the world."

◄ PAUL REVERE

Paul Revere was a highly skilled silversmith, but his great legacy is his famous "Midnight Ride" of April 18, 1775. On that evening, Revere learned of British troop movements from Boston across the Charles River, heading for Lexington and Concord—two hotbeds of Patriot (anti-British) activity. He set off by horse to warn Patriot leaders Samuel Adams and John Hancock in Lexington, and to alert Colonial militias in nearby towns as well. Revere's ride triggered a preplanned alarm network that ultimately sent as many as forty more riders galloping across the countryside, delivering warnings of the British approach.

MARQUIS DE LAFAYETTE ►

His full name was a mouthful: Marie-Joseph Paul Yves Roch Gilbert du Motier, Marquis de Lafayette. Known simply as Lafayette, he was a French officer who famously joined the Americans during the Revolutionary War because he believed theirs to be a righteous cause. Lafayette was just nineteen when he arrived in 1777, but George Washington took an instant liking to the enthusiastic young man and added Lafayette to his staff. The Frenchman was wounded at the Battle of Brandywine and gamely shared the hardship of Washington's troops during the brutal winter at Valley Forge. Later, at the Battle of Monmouth, he witnessed the poor decisions of General Charles Lee and kept Washington informed. The Marquis was also prominently involved in the final battle of the war, the Siege of Yorktown.

◄ SAMUEL ADAMS

This great political philosopher was a primary architect of American principles of government that endure to this day. Adams was the first to openly question the right of British Parliament to tax the colonies without consent, a position that

became the cornerstone of the American Revolution. But he was more than just a thinker—Adams was a leading activist, engaged in the day-to-day coordination of the Patriot resistance movement. No credible historical evidence exists that he helped plan or incite the Boston Tea Party (as portrayed in *Assassin's Creed III*), but he vigorously defended the incident afterward. When British authorities sent forces to arrest Adams in April of 1775, he got early warning thanks to Paul Revere's famous midnight ride. Not long after, he became one of the fifty-six signers of the Declaration of Independence.

THOMAS HICKEY ►

Sergeant Thomas Hickey was a soldier in the Life Guard, a unit assigned to protect the commander in chief, General George Washington. In the spring of 1776, Hickey was caught passing counterfeit money. This led to revelations of an alleged conspiracy by several Life Guard soldiers to defect to the British side and possibly assassinate Washington. The assassination plot was never proven, and may have been merely exaggerated rumor. But Hickey was court-martialed for his plans to defect, found guilty of treason and mutiny, and executed.

◄ BENJAMIN CHURCH

Serving as the chief physician of the Continental Army at the start of the American Revolution, Dr. Benjamin Church secretly sent encrypted letters to the British commander in North America, General Thomas Gage. These notes included extensive intelligence about the strength and deployment of American forces. During the war, only one letter was discovered, and Church made an eloquent defense that saved his life. But other letters to General Gage were found in the twentieth century that confirmed the doctor's treason. In 1778, after his trial, Church was banished from the colonies and allowed to set sail from Boston for Martinique. But his ship disappeared en route and was never heard from again.

KEY LOCATIONS, LANDMARKS, AND EVENTS

PATRIOTS AND LOYALISTS

Not all American colonists wanted to cast off British rule
and turn the colonies into independent, sovereign states.
Colonists who wanted to be free of the king's tyranny called
themselves Patriots. But many Americans valued their
British roots or their connection to British military might.
Called Loyalists, these colonists were wary of independence,
especially in a warlike world where other great seafaring
powers like France, Spain, and the Netherlands could
greatly affect trade routes. Many American merchants and
traders liked the protection that the powerful British Navy
could provide to their shipping concerns.

ABOVE: British soldiers stand guard near the aftermath of the Great
Fire of New York (1776).

RIGHT: Connor leaps from the roof of the Old State House in Boston.
This building appears in the back of Paul Revere's famous engraving of
the Boston Massacre (see opposite page.)

BOSTON

Colonial Boston was a thriving commercial center, with a booming economy that rivaled that of the other two major cities of North America, New York and Philadelphia. But by 1770, the increase in British taxation was taking its toll on Boston's economy, as was the enforced quartering of British Regular troops. The city's strong Puritan roots instilled a culture of thrift and industriousness, as well as a sense of moral outrage at the injustice of British tyranny. Boston also featured a town-meeting style of government that gave its citizens a strong say in civic matters. This autonomy helps explain why the city was at the heart of Colonial resistance to British rule. Many key events in the revolutionary timeline took place there, including the Boston Massacre, the Boston Tea Party, and the Battle of Bunker Hill.

THE BOSTON MASSACRE

Beginning in 1767, the British Parliament passed a series of acts that increased taxation on its North American colonies. Called the Townshend Acts, they were met with strong resistance in Boston. The British responded by sending troops to occupy the city. On March 5, 1770, after two years of tension and protest, a crowd of Boston citizens gathered outside the Old State House to harass the British soldiers on guard there. Things got ugly, and the soldiers opened fire on the protesters, killing five unarmed civilians. Word of the event spread across the colonies, fueling a strong wave of animosity toward the British authorities and nudging America closer to revolt.

PAUL REVERE CREATED THIS FAMOUS ENGRAVING of the Boston Massacre just three weeks after the incident in March of 1770. The dramatic propaganda print quickly flooded the colonies, stirring up strong anti-Crown sentiment, and became one of the most celebrated symbols of the American Revolution.

VALLEY FORGE

After the final battle of 1777, the Continental Army camped for the winter at Valley Forge, Pennsylvania. Unfortunately, Washington's troops were not prepared for the mixture of severe cold and freezing rain. The twelve thousand Continental Army soldiers were poorly clothed, undersupplied, and over-exposed, and even the construction of log huts for shelter couldn't stave off disease and malnutrition. By spring, the army had suffered 2,500 deaths, losing more than a fifth

of its original strength. It was a terrible setback, but it spurred positive action. First, the Continental Congress was so appalled that it swiftly approved funding to upgrade the army supply chain. Second, the soldiers who survived Valley Forge formed a powerful bond—with one another, and with General Washington—plus a hardy streak of perseverance that served them well in the upcoming campaigns. And third, the Continentals gained weeks of valuable training from the demanding Prussian military officer, Friedrich von Steuben, whose close-order drills instilled new confidence and discipline in the demoralized troops.

Connor played a major role in the survival of the soldiers at Valley Forge by helping to recover stolen supplies.

KANIEN'KEHÁ:KA NATION

The easternmost tribe of the Iroquois League was based in the Mohawk Valley in what is today upstate New York, although their hunting territory ranged from Canada down into parts of New Jersey and Pennsylvania. Known as the "Keepers of the Eastern Door," the Kanien'kehá:ka guarded the Iroquois confederacy of tribes against invasion from the east. They were one of four Iroquois tribes that took the British side during the American Revolution. At first, the tribal confederacy tried to remain neutral. But the Crown was their traditional ally, and the British had tried to protect the Iroquois lands from the American colonists after the Seven Years' War. After the American victory, most of the Kanien'kehá:ka people migrated to Canada.

ABOVE: Early concept of Kaniehtí:io, Connor's mother.

THE TOMAHAWK
Tribal warriors often wielded a deadly single-handed axe called the tomahawk. Originally created by the Algonquian Indians before Europeans came to America, the small hatchet could be swung or thrown with great accuracy.

CHAPTER 7

THE FRENCH REVOLUTION

Assassin's Creed: Unity is set during the first five years of the French Revolution, the great upheaval in which the French lower classes rose up and tossed aside the old order of aristocratic rule by bloodline. The story follows the genetic memories of Arno Dorian, a French-Austrian born into nobility in Versailles who eventually becomes a Master Assassin.

ARNO DORIAN

The hero of *Assassin's Creed: Unity,* Arno Dorian is a key figure in legendary historic events like the Storming of the Bastille and the execution of King Louis XVI. Haunted by the deaths of both his Assassin father and adopted Templar father, Arno joins the Brotherhood in an attempt to redeem himself from his past. Joined by Templar Élise de la Serre, Arno works to unravel the mysteries behind the French Revolution.

HISTORICAL OVERVIEW

After the prison governor refused to release the ammunition stores, the mob attacked and captured the Bastille. The governor's head was carried through the streets on a spike.

The French Revolution was certainly a high point in European and world history—a great popular uprising inspired by high-minded ideals. The Declaration of the Rights of Man introduced in 1789 is considered one of the foundations documents in the history of human rights—the basis for a nation of free individuals, equally protected by law. But it was not a clean or peaceful transition of power by any means. Marked by episodes with names like the Reign of Terror, the Day of Daggers, the September Massacres, and the White Terror, the Revolution's historical drama played out as a series of bloody riots, reactions, and reprisals.

THE STORMING OF THE BASTILLE

Often called "the flashpoint of the French Revolution," this event is commemorated every year in France on July 14. The Bastille, an imposing medieval fortress turned prison in the heart of Paris, had come to be seen as a monolithic symbol of French royal tyranny. On July 14, 1789, a mob of protesters rushed into the Bastille's court-yard, demanding the surrender of munitions stored inside. When guards opened fire, killing a hundred rioters, thousands of Parisians flocked to overrun the hated prison. Its capture symbolized the fall of the *ancien régime* (old order) of aristocratic rule, and the incident gave powerful momentum to the French revolutionary cause.

THE REIGN OF TERROR

In September of 1793, the Committee of Public Safety—a group led by Maximilien de Robespierre, operating within the new revolutionary government of France—decided to take harsh action against suspected enemies of the Revolution. Over the next ten months, the term "enemy" was broadened so wide that more than three hundred thousand suspects were arrested, and seventeen thousand were officially executed. Thousands more died in prison or as the result of unofficial "justice." As Robespierre put it, "Softness to traitors will destroy us all." As mastermind of the Reign of Terror, he was powerful, feared . . . and, eventually, hated. It is no surprise that the committee finally turned on Robespierre, making him one of the last victims of the Terror's guillotine in 1794. (See "Robespierre" later in this chapter.)

THE GUILLOTINE
This famous eighteenth century beheading machine was actually designed to be a "humane" form of execution. It became the grisly symbol of the Reign of Terror during the French Revolution.

During the French Revolution, the guillotine was located at what is now known at the Place de la Concorde, not in front of Notre Dame.

HISTORICAL CHARACTERS

Arno finds Germain in his workshop, also the secret location of a hidden room of Templar artifacts.

◀ FRANÇOIS-THOMAS GERMAIN

In the 1700s, the Germain family was a clan of highly skilled craftsmen who had long served as royal silversmiths to the king of France. François-Thomas Germain continued the distinguished tradition after inheriting his father's huge studio, with its staff of eighty workmen. Germain supplied the French royal family with tableware, church silver, lamps, and chandeliers . . . even baby rattles for the royal infants! Unfortunately, in 1765, Germain violated strict regulations of his craft guild by entering into a partnership with bankers to help him collect debts from delinquent customers. The guild expelled him, and thus Germain was dismissed from his post as royal silversmith, ending his radiant career at the young age of thirty-nine. He disappeared from public life and died in obscurity in 1791.

MIRABEAU ▶

Honoré Gabriel Riqueti, Comte de Mirabeau—better known simply as Mirabeau—was a pivotal figure, and a controversial one, in the early days of the French Revolution. He was born into a wealthy merchant family whose members had become "noblemen" by purchasing an aristocratic title. Known as a great orator with a sharp intelligence, Mirabeau was a firm supporter of the monarchy and executive power— and, as it turned out, he was secretly on the king's payroll to help pay off his prodigious personal debts. But when the Revolution began, he became a popular and even beloved voice of the common people. As the crisis intensified and radical elements emerged on both sides, Mirabeau argued eloquently for a compromise position based on a constitutional monarchy like Britain's. But his support waned as extremists like Robespierre rose to power, and Mirabeau's death from a heart infection snuffed out the last great voice of moderation, paving the way for the Reign of Terror.

◀ ROBESPIERRE

Maximilien de Robespierre was a central and highly polarizing figure in the Revolution. His legacy will always be tied closely to the Reign of Terror, during which thousands of his political enemies were executed via guillotine, many with no trial or any other recourse to legal channels for challenging their accusers. An eloquent lawyer and politician, Robespierre started as a fierce advocate for democracy and equal rights for all people, including the poor. He led the effort to abolish slavery in the French colonies and, ironically, he was also a vociferous opponent of the death penalty. But eventually Robespierre would argue for the execution of King Louis XVI and, soon after, would advocate the same dire punishment for the enemies of the Jacobin Club, his political party. His excesses led to a grim backlash that ended with his own head in a basket. Even today, his reputation is hotly debated. Was Robespierre an eloquent spokesman for the oppressed, or a paranoid political bully?

KING LOUIS XVI ▶

Louis was king of France from 1774 until he was officially deposed in 1792 by the new legislative assembly formed during the French Revolution. Although Louis made efforts to abolish serfdom, the *taille* (a land tax on peasantry), and other hated remnants of feudal culture, his reign also coincided with the rise of an inspiring new democracy in America and a general discontent with old ways. (Ironically, Louis XVI was a firm supporter of the Patriot cause in the American Revolution.) On the king's right, the French nobility were hostile to any attempts at reform, and blocked them all; on his left, radical activists were encouraging commoners to question the legitimacy of monarchy and aristocratic privilege. In *Assassin's Creed: Unity,* the entire sequence depicting the opening of the Estates General includes Louis XVI's speech in the background, taken directly from recorded accounts. In the end, his popularity plummeted, and an ill-advised attempt to flee from Paris sealed his fate. Louis XVI was convicted of treason, and his execution in January of 1793 was a truly momentous event, marking the end of more than a thousand years of continuous rule by monarchy in France.

Character art of Louis XVI, France's last monarch before it became a republic. His last words were, "Gentlemen, I am innocent of everything of which I am accused. I hope that my blood may cement the good fortune of the French."

◀ NAPOLÉON BONAPARTE

Few figures in history can match the elevated status of Napoléon Bonaparte. As emperor of France, he led brilliant military campaigns that conquered vast territories across continental Europe. His Napoleonic Code became the foundation for modern legal systems across the world, and he brought the Revolution's enlightened civic ideals to the many lands that he conquered. But Bonaparte started as a young artillery officer trying to negotiate the shifting landscape of the Revolution's early days. Early on, he cast his support to the French republican cause. In 1795, a force of thirty thousand royalist rebels (anti-republican, pro-monarchy) marched on Paris in the "13 Vendémiaire" uprising. Bonaparte engineered a brilliant defense, crushing the royalists with expert artillery placement despite being outnumbered six to one. The victory lifted the young general out of obscurity and made him a national hero of the Revolution.

MARQUIS DE SADE ▶

Donatien Alphonse Francois de Sade lived to be seventy-four years old . . . and spent thirty-two of those years incarcerated, in either prison or a lunatic asylum. In July of 1789, he was languishing in the Bastille, in the twelfth year of imprisonment for numerous scandalous offenses, but was moved out just ten days before the famous storming incident. Within a year he was released, proclaiming himself a champion of the new republic. In an almost unbelievable turn of events, the lifelong aristocrat and deviant pleasure seeker was elected a delegate to the National Convention, assembled to draw up a constitution. But soon the marquis was back in prison again, accused of "moderatism" (of all things) by radicals who supported Robespierre. He was freed after Robespierre was executed, but then arrested again, this time by Napoléon Bonaparte for the obscenity of his writings. De Sade was declared insane and spent the last thirteen years of his life in the Charenton asylum.

KEY LOCATIONS, LANDMARKS, AND EVENTS

PARIS

Paris in the late 1700s was a hotbed of radical thought, dominated by the ideas of the Age of Enlightenment—a philosophical movement centered on notions of reason, liberty, and a belief in science. Parisians had begun to question the legitimacy of royal rule as a birthright, calling for constitutional government based on the will and consent of the people. Many also challenged the rigid traditions and dogmas of the Roman Catholic Church. By 1789, Paris had become the financial and intellectual center of Europe—a teeming capital of commerce, art, fashion, publishing, and architecture with a population of more than six hundred thousand. But economic conditions were becoming more desperate in large segments of the city. The great philosopher Jean-Jacques Rousseau described its crowded eastern neighborhoods: "I saw only narrow, dirty, and foul-smelling streets, villainous black houses with an air of unhealthiness . . . beggars, poverty." These conditions became the fertile soil for the sudden, explosive growth of the French Revolution.

In eighteenth century Paris, the underground tunnel network beneath the city became a renowned "ossuary"—the final resting place of countless numbers of human skeletal remains exhumed from Parisian cemeteries. Today the catacombs hold the remains of more than six million people, with many interior walls made entirely of human skulls and bones!

Concept art of Marie Antoinette at her hamlet on the Versailles Palace grounds

PALACE OF VERSAILLES

As official residence of the French royal family, the Palace of Versailles had been the seat of political power in France for more than a century at the time of the French Revolution. In essence, Versailles functioned as a "micro-state," safely removed from the urban turmoil of Paris. As one of the most opulent buildings in the world, the stunning palace was also seen as a symbol of aristocratic decadence. However, many commoners still believed that the royal family could be a positive, stabilizing force in an unsettling time of radical change. The Women's March on Versailles in October 1789 brought Louis XVI, his family, and most of the French Assembly back to Paris in the hope that the king could work out a constitutional power-sharing deal amongst the other estates.

Louis XVI and Marie Antoinette held "society meals" with up to forty guests served dinner on gold plates and porcelain dishes.

TUILERIES PALACE

The Tuileries Palace served as the Paris residence of French royalty for more than three hundred years. In October of 1789, King Louis XVI and his family were brought from Versailles to the Tuileries, where the Paris-based revolutionary movement could keep an eye on them. On August 10, 1792, as the rebellion raged in the streets of Paris, a huge armed mob stormed the palace and slaughtered the king's Swiss Guard, forcing the royal family to flee to the protection of the National Assembly. This official overthrow of the French monarchy became a major turning point in the Revolution.

Satirical image titled *The plundering of the King's cellar, Paris, 10th August, 1793*, although the actual event took place in 1792.

Concept art of Napoleon and Arno infiltrating Tuileries Palace

THE SEPTEMBER MASSACRES

In the late summer of 1792, panicked rumors began to spread across Paris that French royalists were conspiring with foreign powers to invade the city and restore the old order. Unfortunately, these rumors hinted that the invaders planned to release all political prisoners, who would then join the counter-revolutionary armies. On September 2, armed vigilantes descended on Paris jails and began the mass murder of all inmates, regardless of their crimes. Over the next five days, more than half of the Paris prison population was executed—around 1,400 unarmed detainees, including a number of Catholic priests who had refused to swear an oath to the government for religious reasons. Similar massacres were carried out in a number of other French cities as well.

Although Catholicism was the official religion of France, religious practice was suppressed during the Revolution.

A riot against the French military breaks out on the Paris streets.

108

An estimated 17,000 to 40,000 civilians were executed during the Reign of Terror, about 3,000 lives per month.

THE THERMIDORIAN REACTION

The leadership of Robespierre's political organization, the Jacobin Club, fully supported his Reign of Terror as a political solution. But as the Jacobin zeal for the guillotine spiraled out of control, a strong anti-Jacobin reaction arose in other sectors of the new government. On July 28, 1794, after a wild day and night of accusations and counteraccusations, the assembly sent troops to arrest the "tyrant" Robespierre and his followers. He tried to evade arrest but was shot in the jaw. The prisoners were condemned without judicial process and executed that same day. This event triggered several months of reactionary reprisals called the White Terror that targeted the same radical revolutionary groups who had been so zealous in enforcing the Reign of Terror. Again, hundreds of executions took place without trial.

Read more about Maximilien de Robespierre on page 101.

CHAPTER 8

VICTORIAN LONDON

■

Assassin's Creed: Syndicate is set in the Victorian-era London of 1868. It was a time of relative peace in the world, thanks to the unchallenged sea power and global hegemony of the British Empire, a dominance that lasted almost a full century (1815–1914). So, unlike other Assassin's Creed installments, there is no backdrop of war or violent revolution. But London's bloody underworld provides plenty of strife to make up for that. *Syndicate*'s protagonists are twin Assassins named Evie and Jacob Frye. As the game begins, the siblings are newly arrived in the great and terrible city.

JACOB AND EVIE FRYE

Jacob and Evie Frye arrive in London to free the city from Templar Grand Master Crawford Starrick. They take down the Blighters, a Templar-backed gang, by forming their own criminal syndicate known as the Rooks. More brash and impulsive than his twin sister, Jacob's inclination toward action leads him to focus on eliminating key Templar targets. Dedicated and deadly, Evie is utterly loyal to the tenants of the Creed. She turns her attention to finding the Shroud of Eden, a powerful First Civilization artifact.

HISTORICAL OVERVIEW

Victorian London in 1868 was a city of stunning contrasts. On one hand, it was a time of exhilarating growth. The Industrial Revolution and the Golden Age of Steam had created an explosion of machine technology and commerce that generated vast sums of wealth. Sprawling factories created countless new jobs that brought millions of laborers from rural areas into the city—from 1800 to 1900, London's population exploded from one million to six million people.

These newly manufactured goods, transported swiftly over new railways, transformed British society at every level. As broad new avenues and gleaming architectural symbols of the new era sprang up—the "Big Ben" clock tower, the renovated Buckingham Palace, Trafalgar Square, and the new National Gallery, plus the glittering iron-and-glass Crystal Palace—London rivaled Paris as the world's greatest capital city.

RISE OF THE SLUMS

But the reign of Queen Victoria was also an era of staggering urban poverty. Many of the new industrial barons built their immense fortunes on the backs of a grossly exploited labor force. Factory workers were often little more than indentured servants. In London's unhealthy, overcrowded slums, residents slogged through a labyrinth of narrow, foul-smelling streets filled with festering sewage. Poor sanitation created a never-ending series of cholera outbreaks. Tons of untreated industrial waste were dumped directly into the River Thames.

Abject poverty, discontent, class resentment—it all combined to spur writers like Charles Dickens and Karl Marx to question this system of economic inequality. It also created a perfect setting for the rise of organized crime. A vast underclass began to gaze up at the privileged few and ask: Why?

HISTORICAL CHARACTERS

CHARLES DICKENS ▶

Critics and scholars have called him the "literary colossus of his age." Considered the greatest novelist of the Victorian era—and certainly one of the greatest of any era—Charles Dickens was the author of such lasting literary classics as *Oliver Twist*, *David Copperfield*, *A Christmas Carol*, *A Tale of Two Cities*, and *Great Expectations*. A profound social critic, Dickens despised the inequality of Victorian society, and his work was full of withering commentary. As a powerful advocate for the poor and destitute, Dickens often included unflinching portrayals of squalor and desperate poverty.

◀ CHARLES DARWIN

Charles Darwin was not only a great scientist but also one of the most widely influential figures in human history. In his brilliant treatise *On the Origin of Species* (1859), the English naturalist posited his theory (backed by abundant evidence) of "natural selection," in which the struggle of all species for survival dictates the course of evolution. His argument was so thorough and compelling that by the 1870s, the wider scientific community and the educated public had accepted it as fact. His examination of the biological mechanisms that create the abundant diversity of life had a profound effect on almost every other field of inquiry, including economics and the study of human behavior.

ALEXANDER GRAHAM BELL ▶

This great Scottish scientist, engineer, and inventor devised and patented the first working telephone. In 1868, Bell was just twenty-one, but he had spent much of his youth fascinated by sound, and was already working on the transmission of human speech by electrical means. Bell left Victorian London for Canada in 1870 after a series of family tragedies—he lost both of his brothers to tuberculosis. His first successful telephone transmission was in 1874 at his lab in Boston.

THE FIRST TELEPHONE

The first successful transmission of clear speech between two devices occurred on March 10, 1876, when Alexander Graham Bell spoke into a transmitter to his assistant Thomas Watson: "Mr. Watson, come here, I want to see you!" The vibrations of the call traveled via magneto-electric currents to a receiver in another room, where Watson heard Bell's "voice" emerge.

RIGHT: Photograph of the Bell liquid telephone receiver

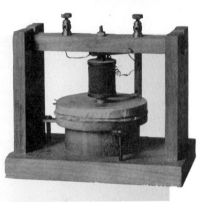

FLORENCE NIGHTINGALE ▶

Known as "The Lady with the Lamp"—the compassionate nurse making her night rounds of wounded soldiers during wartime—Florence Nightingale was a cultural icon in Victorian London. Widely considered the founder of modern nursing, she introduced the concept of a professional nurse corps with rigorous medical training. But Nightingale was also a social reformer who worked to improve conditions for all sectors of society. Her causes included health education, medical hygiene, hunger relief for the poor, workplace safety and fairness, and city sanitation issues.

◀ KARL MARX

This German thinker's socioeconomic and political theories became some of the most influential in history. His arguments were based on the idea of class struggle between the ruling class (the bourgeoisie) that owns or controls the means of production (factories, businesses, etc.) and the working class (the proletariat) that provides labor for those ventures in exchange for wages. Marx believed that the workers would eventually rise up and seize control of production to create a socialist state and, eventually, a "classless," communist society. Even countries that rejected socialism and communism as political alternatives were affected by Marx's ideas on the value of labor and the self-destructive danger of class-based inequality. In 1849, Marx moved to Victorian London, where he published a pamphlet entitled *The Communist Manifesto*, and wrote his masterwork, the three-volume *Das Kapital*. In 1868, he was a passionate advocate for workers. He remained in the city until his death in 1883.

THE LONDON SPEECHES OF KARL MARX in the Assassin's Creed: Syndicate are not actual historical moments, but the words spoken come directly from Marx's *The Communist Manifesto*. For example: "Proletarians of all lands, unite!"

QUEEN VICTORIA

Born Alexandrina Victoria of the House of Hanover, she became Queen in 1837 at age eighteen and reigned for sixty-three years. The term "Victorian" often refers to her conservative standards of personal morality. But the Victorian era was also a dynamic time in British history, bringing significant and often volatile change to all aspects of British life. In 1868, Victoria was still in seclusion after the devastating loss of her beloved husband, Prince Albert. For nearly a quarter-century after his death, Victoria avoided public appearances and rarely set foot in London. But the new prime minister elected that year, Benjamin Disraeli, had become a favorite of the queen.

◄ BENJAMIN DISRAELI

Benjamin Disraeli was an English politician who served two separate terms as prime minister of the United Kingdom. The first term, in 1868, began when he stepped in after his party leader, the Earl of Derby, retired. It lasted less than a year. In that short time, however, he developed a close friendship with Queen Victoria that lasted until he died in 1881. His main achievement during this first term was passage of the Corrupt Practices Act, designed to prevent the most egregious forms of electoral fraud and bribery.

JAMES BRUDENELL, SEVENTH EARL OF CARDIGAN ►

Brudenell was a wealthy aristocrat who, as a politician, fought hard to preserve the privileges of the noble class against the initiatives of democratic reformists. Using the British Army's practice of allowing purchase of commissions, he became a cavalry officer and soon "worked" his way up to the rank of lieutenant colonel in command of a regiment during the Crimean War. In the Battle of Balaclava, he led them on a tragic charge made famous by Alfred, Lord Tennyson, the British poet laureate, in his narrative poem "The Charge of the Light Brigade." After Brudenell retired from the military, he spent much time on his expensive yacht and continued his political activity. He died in March of 1868 after falling from his horse, possibly the result of a stroke.

◄ FREDERICK ABBERLINE

In 1868, Abberline was a sergeant in the Y Division of London's Metropolitan Police Service, based in the city's Highgate district. Five years later he would be promoted to Inspector and transferred to the H Division in Whitechapel. In 1888, when a serial string of grisly killings in the grimy, downtrodden district became the most infamous murder case of all time, Abberline was placed in charge of the detective team. The infamous Jack the Ripper preyed on at least five (and possibly more) female prostitutes who worked London's East End slums. Widespread newspaper coverage of the sensational slayings contributed to the growing legend of the Ripper. Unfortunately, Abberline's official investigation never managed to unravel the twisted threads of evidence.

LOCATIONS, LANDMARKS, AND EVENTS

1860s LONDON UNDERWORLD

Life could be brutal in the Victorian-era slums of London's East End, some of the most infamous hellholes in history. By 1868, once-respectable areas like the Whitechapel district had become overcrowded, unsanitary "rookeries" where a new and widespread urban criminal class could operate with impunity as the result of lax police oversight. Gangs arose as a form of protection amid desperate poverty and dog-eat-dog life on the streets. Over time, some gangs grew into more sophisticated crime syndicates with organized control of illegal activities on their own turf of boroughs in the East End.

LAMBETH ASYLUM

In the nineteenth century, the infamous Bethlem Hospital—more commonly known as "Bedlam"—housed many of England's most difficult and dangerous lunatics, as mentally ill patients were called then. Notorious for inhumane conditions, the facility was built along Lambeth Road, and thus was sometimes called the Lambeth Asylum.

Henry Mayhew, a journalist who pushed for housing reform, wrote of the slums: "The air has literally the smell of a graveyard . . . The water is covered with a scum almost like a cobweb, and prismatic with grease."

ALHAMBRA THEATRE

Located in the West End of London, the Alhambra served as a popular theater and music hall in 1868. It was originally built as a hall for art and science exhibitions called the Royal Panopticon. By 1864, the structure was transformed into the Alhambra Music Hall, where musical performances mixed with ballet, aerial acts, and light opera. It also featured a bar, the Promenade, where patrons could sip champagne and mix with the dance troupe's backup dancers, called the corps de ballet.

In *Assassin's Creed: Syndicate*, Alhambra Music Hall is refurbished by gang leader Maxwell Roth. After a performance entitled Corvus the Trickster, Roth sets the theater on fire with the audience still inside in an attempt to kill Jacob Frye.

Romanticism-style concept art of the palace grounds

Read more about Queen
Victoria on page 116.

BUCKINGHAM PALACE

Originally built as a townhouse for the Duke of Buckingham in 1703, the structure was expanded in the 1800s into a grand, 775-room palace with three wings built around a central courtyard. When Queen Victoria took the throne in 1837, Buckingham Palace became the official London residence of the British monarch. But after her husband, Prince Albert, died in 1861, a grieving Victoria retired to her country castles, shunning the London scene. By 1868, she had started making occasional appearances in the London residence, but the palace still remained shuttered for most of the year.

ST. PAUL'S CATHEDRAL

This imposing, domed baroque structure sits on the highest point in the City of London and is considered the "mother church" of the Diocese of London. Built in the early 1700s to replace the old St. Paul's, which had been gutted by the Great Fire of London in 1666, it features a dome that had become one of the most recognizable and celebrated architectural wonders in the world by 1868.

MONUMENT TO THE GREAT FIRE OF LONDON

COMPLETED IN 1677, this 202-foot-tall fluted Doric column was built to commemorate the Great Fire of London, a massive conflagration that devastated the city eleven years earlier. That firestorm destroyed thirteen thousand homes, eighty-seven churches—including the original St. Paul's Cathedral—and even threatened the king's Palace of Whitehall. In 1868, the towering monument was one of the most recognizable features of the London skyline. Inside, a winding staircase of 311 steps led to a small observation deck at the top.

TOWER OF LONDON

The Tower of London is rich in history. The fortress is a complex of buildings trimmed with battlements and corner towers. In its center, the formidable keep known as the White Tower rises prominently and somewhat ominously. Built by William the Conqueror in 1078, it was fashioned as a maximum-security royal residence. Over its lifetime, however, the White Tower became equally renowned as a high-profile prison. By 1868, the Tower of London was used primarily as a garrison for troops. Its historical significance also made it a tourist attraction, and Prince Albert himself (husband of Queen Victoria) oversaw renovations to restore much of the structure's original medieval flavor.

Throughout history, thirty-five Yeoman Warders guard the Tower of London at one time, headed up by a Constable of the Tower.

IMAGES

Assassin's Creed Artists: Fernando Acosta, David Alvarez, Daniel Atanasov , Gilles Beloeil, Eddie Bennun, J. Bigorne, Martin Deschambault, Patrick Desgreniers, Maxime Desmesttre, Thierry Doizon, Vincent Gaigneux, Yuriy Georgiev, Grant Hillier, Diana Kalugina, Ivan Koritarev, Raphaël Lacoste, Patrick Lambers, David Levy, Olivier Martin, Borislav Mitkov, Khai Nguyen, T. Nguyen, Hugo Puzzuoili, Max Qin, Yu Li Qing, Ludovic Ribardiere, Kobe Sek, Tony Zhou Shou, Caroline Soucy, Yong Jin Teo, Remko Troost, Stéphane Turgeon, Jan Urschel, William Wu, Nacho Yagüe, Donglu Yu, and Darek Zabrocki.

ADDITIONAL IMAGE SOURCES

Page 24: Pierre, Jacotin. *Acre, Nazareth, le Jourdain*. Map. [Paris], 1818. New York Public Library Digital Collections.

Page 29: Unknown artist. *Young artists in the funeral chapel of the Medici*. Engraving. [Paris], 1867. From Magasin Pittoresque.

Page 34: Collier, John. *A Glass of Wine with Caesar Borgia*. Painting. [London], 1914. From *Daily Telegraph, King Albert's Book*, page 152.

Page 43: di Giovanna, Bertoldo. *Bertoldo di giovanni, medaglia della congiura dei pazzi (lorenzo)*. Medal. [Italy], 1478. Photo courtesy of Sailko.

Page 76: Unknown artist. *Mount Vernon*. Print. [Unknown location], No Date Recorded on Shelflist Card. Library of Congress.

Page 77: The ruins of Fort William Henry.

Page 79: Bobbett, Albert and Felix Octavius Carr Darley. *Montcalm Trying to Stop the Massacre*. Photographic Print. [Unknown location], 1870. Library of Congress.

Page 89 (top right): Berger, D. *Boston Tea-Party. Three Cargoes of Tea Destroyed*. Print. [Unknown location], 1784. Library of Congress.

Page 91: Revere, Paul. *The bloody massacre perpetrated in King Street Boston on March 5th 1770 by a party of the 29th Regt. Boston*. Image. [Boston], 1770. Library of Congress.

Page 92: Unknown artist. *The ragged and defeated Continental Army marching to the encampment at Valley Forge*, winter of 1777–78. Lithograph. [Unknown location], 19th century.

Page 107: Zoffany, Johan and Richard Earlom. *The plundering of the King's cellar, Paris, 10th August, 1793 (i.e., 1792)*. Image. [London], 1795. Library of Congress.

Page 115: Illustration of Florence Nightengale during the Crimean War

Page 116: Painting of Queen Victoria and Prince Albert in 1843

All rights reserved. Published by Scholastic Inc., *Publishers since 1920*. SCHOLASTIC and associated logos are trademarks and/or registered trademarks of Scholastic Inc.

ISBN 978-1-338-09914-0 (TRADE)
ISBN 978-1-338-13376-9 (SSE)

10 9 8 7 6 5 4 3 2 1   16 17 18 19 20 21

Printed in the U.S.A. 40
First printing 2016

INSIGHT EDITIONS
PUBLISHER: Raoul Goff
ACQUISITIONS MANAGER: Robbie Schmidt
ART DIRECTOR: Chrissy Kwasnik
DESIGNERS: *tabula rasa* graphic design
EXECUTIVE EDITOR: Vanessa Lopez
ASSOCIATE EDITOR: Katie DeSandro
PRODUCTION EDITOR: Rachel Anderson
PRODUCTION MANAGER: Thomas Chung

With thanks to the Assassin's Creed team: Aymar Azaïzia, Anouk Bachman, Antoine Ceszynski, Maxime Durand, Caroline Lamache